Beloved reader,

# HOW THE PUBLIC SCHOOL SYSTEM STOLE

## PETEY GUZMAN'S LIFE

E. A. Hults Elko

authorHOUSE®

Enjoy this labor of love – and find out the truth about public education!! Best, E.A. Hults Elko

AuthorHouse™
1663 Liberty Drive
Bloomington, IN 47403
www.authorhouse.com
Phone: 1 (800) 839-8640

Published by AuthorHouse  04/29/2015

ISBN: 978-1-5049-0827-6 (sc)
ISBN: 978-1-5049-0828-3 (hc)
ISBN: 978-1-5049-0826-9 (e)

Library of Congress Control Number: 2015906407

Print information available on the last page.

*Dedicated to*

*My family & friends, whose love and support is a blessing*
*Fellow teachers, whose life's work is honorable, noble, and heroic*
*Today's students, whose voices must be heard*

# CHAPTER 1

High school sucks. I mean, *really* sucks. I love how everyone always looks at teenagers and says shit like, "Oh, kids don't know how good they have it. Those are the best years of your life." Really? Then your life must really suck as an adult if you're saying that.

Not that you really give a shit, but I'm gonna start telling this story with some background from both my freshman and sophomore years. I'm not through my junior year yet, but you gotta be clear on the last two years in order to understand where I'm at right now—and why I would probably consider the start of this year as the official "beginning of the end."

The first thing you gotta know about is Ms. Moore. She was my freshman English teacher. When I walked in to her class the first day two years ago, I thought she was kinda nuts—a little too much caffeine for a woman in her forties. I mean, really, the woman never sat still. It was somewhat exhausting watching her flutter about the room. But as much as I liked to rip on her, I can safely say she was my favorite teacher—not only freshman year, but ever.

Usually teachers are just these drones that bark orders and get all pissy when you so much as stare at them blankly. Ms. Moore wasn't like that. And I was kinda surprised that she wasn't. I think she was one of the longest-employed teachers at our high school. Twenty-two years or something like that. But you would've thought she was fresh out of college, full of excitement and energy. At first I wanted to hate her because people like that generally annoy me. Usually when there's hype about someone or something, I'm the first to be the naysayer. But she made it hard to hate her. It was like she genuinely *cared*—about a lot of things: English, literature, grammar, spelling, big vocabulary words, Shakespeare. But beyond those, she made it seem like she cared about *us* the most.

She used to make us write these journals—I know, typical English teacher, right? But these were different. It wasn't stupid like, *write about your thoughts on immigration* or something. She actually wanted us to write *to her*—all the time. About anything. We had to submit journals to her at least once a week. We could write about anything—how we hated her class, how much reading books sucked, if we hated our parents, which college football teams should make the playoffs, whatever. I guess she just wanted us writing for the sake of writing. Since there were ten weeks in a marking period, we had to submit ten different entries. If you had all ten, it counted as a 100 test grade. But you could always submit more. In fact, she encouraged it. I thought it was kinda weird at the time, but I figured it wasn't that hard to write some shit about myself once a week for a freebie test grade. I'm kinda a slacker anyway, so I could use all the help I could get—especially if it was an easy *A*.

The first weekend following the first week of school, I told my mom I needed to go out and get one of those marble composition notebooks—you know, those stupid-looking notebooks with the black and white covers? It was actually kinda satisfying to see the look on my mom's face; it was like she couldn't believe her kid was asking to go out to buy *school supplies.*

Mom's always been my rock. She's kinda the cutest little Puerto-Rican woman you've ever seen—probably not even 5'1", belly so round you could roll her down the street, ocean-blue eyes, jet black wavy hair. She and my real dad were seriously the American dream. Grew up in Puerto Rico, came to the U.S. as teenagers—not speaking a lick of English—and worked in restaurants until they saved enough money to buy their first house.

My mom eventually got a job as a cashier in our local supermarket. My dad got a job at the Port Authority. I wish he hadn't taken it. He died in the Twin Towers on 9/11. I was only three. People say that three-year-olds are too young to understand the shit going on around them, but that's not true. I remember the footage they kept showing on TV, the plane crash, the smoke. I remember my mom falling to her knees, tears streaming down her face, holding me while sobbing. I remember her perfume-smelling hair when she pressed her head into my shoulder, squeezing me more tightly than one should a three-year-old.

I think she worried that I wouldn't have a father figure, so it was only like two years before she remarried some dude named Ricardo. That's my stepdad. I fucking hate him. It's a long story, and I really don't wanna get into it right now, but trust me. He's a douche.

At the end of the first marking period freshman year, I actually submitted thirteen entries to Ms. Moore. I surprised even myself that

I had done the assignment—and actually more than was required. A week after I turned in my notebook, we were working on some activity when Ms. Moore asked me to come up to her desk for a moment. She smiled, and handed back my ratty-looking journal— evidence I had actually used the thing.

"Petey," she said so softly I had to strain my ears, "this was outstanding. I loved reading your entries. You have a lot to say, and you have an important story to tell. I want you to keep writing— every day, if you can. And know that if you ever want to talk about the things you've been writing, I'm here for you."

I didn't really say anything, except to kinda nod and take back my notebook. I went back to my desk and started thumbing through the pages to see if she had written anything. I was shocked to see that the pages were covered in pink gel-type ink (the kind that smears if you don't give it enough time to dry). This woman had put comments all throughout the pages—not just like, circlings of misspellings…I'm talking advice, questions, exclamations, etc. It was like an interactive back-and-forth exchange. You would've thought that our communication had been a text message conversation. I couldn't believe she had spent what looked like a *lot* of time writing back to me. I mean, did she write this much for everyone? I would've assumed so since she always went on and on about how much she loved us. But if that was the case, I could say with certainty that this woman *definitely* didn't have a life.

Regardless, it intrigued me enough to keep writing—and to try to meet the challenge she had given me to write every day. I didn't always have time to, but I probably averaged like three or four times a week. Because of the back-and-forth nature of the journals, there was always something to write about. I was never lacking material. Sometimes several pages would get sucked up just responding to one of the many questions Ms. Moore had asked me in a previous entry. Her questions often served as future writing prompts for me to offer my response.

Eventually, I started to stop by and see Ms. Moore. We'd chat about my entries, her feedback, and class. She always seemed to drop whatever she was doing and just *listen*. It was kinda weird—almost like she was a therapist or something. But it felt good that someone cared. With my mom always picking up shifts at the store, and the fact that I pretty much never spoke to my stepdad, Ms. Moore was like having a second parent—a second mom. She always gave great advice—but only if I asked. She was careful about offering advice that I didn't ask for.

The more we talked, the more I wrote. I wanted to make her proud—to live up to her expectations. I found myself submitting a collection of new entries every week or so, which was way before assignment deadlines. I thought most of my writing was pretty surface-level. But for whatever reason, it seemed like Ms. Moore thought I had more to say. I actually probably did. But I was never one to trust people in authority, so I stuck to what I thought were pretty safe topics.

Freshman year passed quickly for the most part. On the last day of school, I asked Ms. Moore if I could turn my journals into e-mails that I sent her instead of handing them in (since I wouldn't be able to tangibly put them in the class drop-box over the summer). She agreed, and I was pleased to get an e-mail back from her pretty much once a week throughout the summer.

Toward the end of summer, Ms. Moore wrote that I was welcome to continue writing to her (back in hard-copy/notebook format) once the school year began. I started to wonder if she did this for all of her students…I mean, what if someone from twenty-two years ago was still writing to her? How could she possibly keep up? Mom took me to get a brand new composition book, which was now my fourth. (I had gone through three my freshman year, if you could believe it… I know, I know—I could hardly believe it myself). Mom recognized how much I had been writing, and seemed pleased that I actually had a non-violent hobby for a teenage boy. I think she was also psyched that I had another trusted adult around that I could talk to—it seemed to take some of the pressure off her as the "full-time" mom. She had met Ms. Moore at mid-year conferences, and was thrilled I was not only *passing*, but maintaining an *A* average in the class. I'm almost ashamed to admit how much I enjoyed writing in that damn journal. By the time sophomore year began, eleven pages were already full, ready to hand in to Ms. Moore even though she was no longer my current-year English teacher.

I popped in to see her the first day that year during my lunch period, ready to turn in my entries. I was a little surprised that she seemed pretty distracted. I mean, I'm not kidding when I say the woman always used to literally *stop* what she was doing and give me her full attention. I guess I had grown a bit spoiled about that. But it seemed an unlikely coincidence that just as I was getting ready to start digging a little deeper and disclosing more of my life to her, she wasn't all there. I thought maybe she was just having an off day. I wish I had known then what I know now—cuz little did I know that the disappointment I felt that day was only going to increase as the year went on.

# CHAPTER 2

It is with the deepest regret of my life that I begin this journal. I am ashamed to even talk about this, but if I don't bring these things to light, I won't be able to live with myself. All I can hope is that the reason I'm here today is to tell this story so that someone can learn from it. Let this be a warning to public school teachers and parents everywhere. The system is stealing our kids. It's a "wolf in sheep's clothing" claiming to care about our children. But something is very wrong. We have to fight back. I'm here to tell you the truth about what's been going on. Let me start from the beginning. Let me tell you the story about Petey Guzman.

I have been teaching for twenty-two years at the same high school. I *love* my job. (Actually, that's not true. I *used* to love it—when it was pure). Teaching for me used to be about reaching kids. Sure, we had to teach content and curriculum, but mostly, we were here for the kids. I mean, let's face it: we've got kids coming to school today with all sorts of baggage, whether it's divorced parents, or violence in the home, or no support system. The list goes on and on. Before teachers can teach *anything*, they have to be a kid's advocate, on the kid's side. The kids have to "buy in" to you—they have to know that you love them and have their back. Otherwise, they're not gonna give a hoot about geometry or Shakespeare. If they care about you, though, and you truly care about them, they'll do anything for you (and they come to realize you'll do anything for *them*, too).

Years ago, you used to actually be able to teach *and* be there for kids. It was with such pride that you knew you weren't just there to teach the kids topics in academia; you could teach them about *life*, too. Over the years, I've had countless conversations with students about how their boyfriend broke up with them, their locker was jammed, their parents didn't understand, their class schedule was awful, the cafeteria food was insipid (ok, they didn't use that word—I did). The thing is though, we teachers could be a second trusted adult that the kids could go to and count on. (Note: I'm aware that as an English teacher, I just ended the previous sentence in a preposition, but please, spare me. I don't have time to worry about minor details right now when there's so much at stake). Give it time—I'm sure I won't be able to finish this story without sharing my utter disdain for certain people—like the politicians who don't know a thing about how to teach kids, or those folks in upper and middle management drinking the same Kool-Aid—most of whom are overly pedantic, pretentious, and condescending. I mean, really, people are people. How hard is it to treat others warmly and respectfully? Stop acting like you're "above" *anyone*—you're not. No one wants to sit around and listen to these so-called "leaders" pontificate and bloviate about how smart they are. (And if they're reading this, they probably just had to stop to look up the word *bloviate* anyway). And yet these are the people making decisions that ruin the lives of kids like Petey Guzman. It makes me so angry I can hardly see straight. (Oops. See? There I go again. Ok, I'm climbing down from the soapbox now).

Anyway, that's how we *used* to be able to teach. The education profession was about more than just exposing kids to important works from the literary canon. Today, however, we've been forced to do things differently…which is why the public school system was able to steal Petey Guzman's life.

I need for others to heed this tale. I'm not one to offer advice unsolicited, but I implore you to listen at least long enough to understand what happened and *why* it happened. I never thought I'd be sharing a story like this…I honestly planned on being 87-years-old still putting pink comments on students' papers (so long as I was coherent!). My goal was never to make everyone out there super-paranoid or overly suspicious of the hands who care for their kids at school. I mean, in all seriousness, I feel like I'm telling you the public school system version of Orwell's *1984*. (Although it would be fun to come up with a new book title for that, wouldn't it? I can just see it… *Schooled: The Truth about Public Education* or *Dismissed: Why Teachers Can't Reach or Teach Anymore*). Sarcasm aside, I can't ignore this story. I mean, maybe I am just doing this as a catharsis because I blame myself. But whatever the reason, it's a story worth hearing and I've got to tell it. I can't be silent anymore. Everyone deserves to know the truth. So much for being an 87-year-old educator… After what I've witnessed, it seems that "early retirement" would be the safest choice for everyone.

# CHAPTER 3

"Oh! Petey! You startled me," Ms. Moore said, glancing up from her work. She was seated at her desk, surrounded by what looked like several stacks of paperwork. She looked at me almost guiltily, apologetically. Then her eyes fell on to my newly purchased marble composition notebook and I thought I saw a flash of panic cross her face. I took it almost as if she was pissed, kinda like, *Oh, great—I got enough shit to do and this kid wants to drop off a notebook all about his life. I don't have time for this.* But almost as soon as the thought flashed through my mind, Ms. Moore stood up and walked over to me, smiling warmly.

"Hi, sweetie," she said, reaching out her arms to hug me. "Good to see you. How's it feel being back?"

"Good, good," I said, somewhat muffled in the embrace. "I wish I had you again this year. Last year with you was awesome."

"I'm sure your sophomore year will be a great one, too," she responded kindly.

"Geez, are you already that swamped? There's no way you could have that much grading to do already, right?" I asked, pointing to the piles on her desk.

"No," she sighed, sounding overwhelmed. "Actually, these papers have nothing to do with my new students. I *wish* they were piles of student work I had assigned. They're—" she stopped, seeming to reprimand herself. "They're just requirements from the state and the district."

"Oh," I said, feeling kinda like a schmuck to be adding to her load. I held up my notebook. "So you probably don't have time to read this, then, huh? I've got a fresh eleven pages for you from the tail-end of summer," I smiled, hopeful.

"Oh, Petey, I always have time for you. Can you leave it on my desk? I just gotta run some errands now, but I'll get to it."

It was kinda a weird request to leave it on her desk. We always left our journals in the class drop-box, but as I glanced around the room, I didn't see it anywhere. I guess with her being buried under that load of paperwork, maybe she hadn't gotten a chance to put it out yet.

"I think you're gonna really like this set. I took your advice and 'dug deep' just like you said." I paused, feeling kinda guilty. "I appreciate you still doing this even though I don't have you anymore."

She looked at me sternly. "Hey—you *remember* what I told you guys. I'm not just your teacher freshman year, but *always*. I'm so happy you've kept journaling, Petey. I can't wait to see what you've written."

She started to head for her door which I took as my cue to leave, so I finally dropped the notebook onto her desk and then followed her out. I'm not gonna lie; it had been a bit of an awkward encounter. But then again, it *was* the first day back. I mean, I don't blame the woman for not having a clean desk. It's just that this set of entries was important. I had started to go a bit beneath the surface. Last week, my stupid stepdad and I had one of those explosive arguments we're notorious for having (over laundry this time), and I had written it all down. It sucked up like five pages in my notebook and seriously, I write hella small. I wanted to tell Ms. Moore about myself, about my life. I guess I also wanted to offer her some justification as to why some days I had probably come into her class moody and pissed off last year. I figured if I told her some of that, it might explain some of my behavior. I'm not sure why it mattered to tell her all that now, but I felt like I should—like she deserved to know. Plus, she was trustworthy and always understood.

I passed Ms. Moore's classroom a few times later that week. Each time I glanced through the glass window of her door, she was at her desk, face buried in paperwork. I was actually shocked that during some of those times, there were actually *students* in the room. Like I said, Ms. Moore was one of the craziest, most energetic teachers I've ever seen in my life. If there were kids in her room, she was up and about—*always* amidst them. She was *never* at her own desk. It used to be a running joke that whenever an administrator or another adult came into the room, it'd always take 'em a while to find her cuz she blended right in with the kids. I'm telling you, she was never at her desk. That was way too "teachery" for her.

But even though things seemed a bit different this year, I didn't have a leg to stand on when my journal was ready for me a week later (as was usually promised). I popped in to see Ms. Moore on my way to lunch, once again interrupting her as she was hunched over her desk.

"Ms. Moore?" I whispered, barely audible. I was afraid of scaring the shit out of her again.

"Hey, Petey," she replied, not yet looking up.

"Uh, sorry to uh, interrupt, but I was just wondering if you finished responding to my journal yet?"

"Oh, sure, hon—it's over there in the outbox," she said, flicking her wrist in the general direction. "Feel free to grab it. And keep doing what you're doing. I like what I'm hearing."

I wandered over to the outbox bin for journal retrievals, glancing back as I did. This was *really* weird. I don't know what came over me, but all of a sudden I felt really *sorry* for her. She looked frustrated, annoyed, sad, and hopeless all rolled in to one. It was so strange. I also found it kinda creepy that she hadn't looked up at all the whole time, but knew it was me. Talk about going through the motions. In nanoseconds, my brain started guessing at possible targets.

What do old people complain about? I've heard them bitch about like, marital issues, their kids, the work they're having done on their house (like, "oh, we're redoing our kitchen" blah blah), and shit having to do with like their mortgage companies or whatever. (I'm still not even sure what a mortgage company is). But Ms. Moore always had it all together. It's not like she went on and on about her own life with us, but when she *would* let us in on her life (which we all really liked about her since teachers *rarely* did that), her stories were uplifting, funny, and sometimes just plain poking fun at herself and her own family in a playful way. She was always super-real with us. And we loved that about her. Whatever type of personal story she would share in a given class, it was something we could learn from. And she was practically *always* a happy camper. I don't think I ever saw her in a bad mood. The only time she ever seemed upset was if there was something that negatively affected us kids (whether it was massive like world news or local like a school board decision). That's what I mean about her loving us. We all knew she did, which is probably why she was so well-liked. Trust me, I knew some of the kids Ms. Moore had in her class over the years. She's had to teach some *real* assholes (some of whom were my friends, I'll admit). But honestly, they all fucking *loved* her. Nobody I knew ever spoke ill of Ms. Moore.

So I'm not gonna lie, I felt kinda sad looking at her as I picked up my notebook and turned to go. I mean, I knew it probably wasn't about me and more about some stupid adult shit, but still. Ms. Moore rarely looked unhappy, but it looked like that was gonna be the new norm. I sensed a bit of a pity party I was gonna be throwing for myself, too. It's hard to put my finger on it, but I guess I felt like, *dismissed.* It's not necessarily that I felt like she *didn't* care, but it's almost like she didn't have *time* to care. Just seemed really weird.

When I left Ms. Moore's, I went to the library to read her responses. (I know it's probably shocking—*me*, going to the library—but I liked to read her feedback as soon as I got it, and the cafeteria was way too loud to concentrate). That's actually one of the cool things I'd say I like about my school. Lunch is like this flex-period where the whole school stops and you can go wherever you want. Some people shoot hoops in the gym, some meet with teachers for extra help, some see their club advisors about activities, and some go to the library. I mean, you can of course eat in the cafeteria, but the overall student body does a pretty good job of spreading themselves out among the options—and it varies on any given day.

I smiled when I opened the front cover of my notebook and was greeted by pink gel ink. Sure enough, the pages were still covered with Ms. Moore's comments, feedback, and questions. It sounds really corny, but it was kind of like getting a warm hug from someone you hadn't seen in years. I mean, I know my own process of writing was probably like "therapeutic" or some bullshit, but even better was reading the pink. That's where it was like you knew someone got you. They heard you. They understood where you were coming from. Ms. Moore got it. She got me. It was pretty cool. Sometimes I had to reread her comments a few times cuz they were written in cursive. (I'm not so great at cursive. I always print. And my penmanship sucks. It always impressed me that Ms. Moore could read my writing. She could read *anything*. Even though there's no way in hell I'd ever be smart enough to become a doctor, I definitely had the handwriting to match). That's another thing that's kinda freaky about Ms. Moore: she could seriously decode *anyone's* handwriting. With computers and typed work, I think teachers don't see as many handwritten assignments, but Ms. Moore could decipher handwriting so well, they could have used her for crime scene investigations. I mean, even if someone didn't put their *name* on their work, she knew whose it was. It was a commonly known fact that she possessed this talent. Actually, there was one time a kid challenged her about this ability, making some random remark that she couldn't be *that* good at it— that she couldn't possibly know off-hand what everyone's individual writing looked like. She proceeded sweetly, describing to him his *own* handwriting right down to the way he made capital B's. It was amazing. In that moment, you couldn't help but feel like, *Yeah. Go get him, Ms. Moore. You're my hero.*

Anyway, I wasn't disappointed. Based on her recent strange behavior, I thought Ms. Moore's comments would have been sparse or less than what they'd usually been. But they weren't. I was pleasantly surprised. At the end of the entries, she had written her typical long-ass note, which usually recapped everything, offered some insight, and requested something. Her last three lines on the page, scrawled at the bottom said, *Thanks for digging deeper. I applaud your openness—especially regarding Ricky. It helps to process your feelings. Keep it up. I'd love to read more.* I was happy she'd noticed and paid attention to the whole stepdad drama. I'm pretty sure she had always gotten the feeling I couldn't stand him, but it was nice to start opening up about that stuff. And it felt great having someone on my side.

Maybe I had misjudged Ms. Moore. Maybe she was totally fine, just busy. I shifted myself on the library couch, scooched my legs up beneath me, and dug into my pocket for a pen. I took off the pen cap and fitted it into the end of its rod before drawing a line across the page to start a new entry. I then scribbled a fresh date on the right, just under the line. I usually did that to save paper instead of starting on the top of a fresh page. Oh, and I *always* wrote in blue pen, which was kinda funny cuz Ms. Moore used to tell us all the time that she hated blue pen and writing that was in blue ink. Definitely a woman with opinions. (I guess she must've really loved me, though, if she was always willing to read my pages covered in blue!). Yeah, that actually was a good point. Maybe I *had* just been overreacting. Maybe nothing was bothering Ms. Moore.

# CHAPTER 4

What I was trying to begin telling you about before I got going on my rant was the story of Petey Guzman, one of those students who left an indelible mark upon me as an educator. He is what I would call one of my "breakthrough" students, having influenced me as many others have over the last twenty-two years. Petey is one of those kids I often identify early on—remarkable potential, yet standing on such a delicate sewer grate, he could easily fall through the cracks at any moment.

I live for students like that. It is my *mission* in life to reach those kids. That's what I was put on this planet to do. I make it my business to reach *all* of my kids, but some of them are harder to get to (which is why I title them my "breakthrough" kids). Petey was a dead giveaway for one of these right from the very beginning.

In the first month of his freshman year, we had to give a district-wide "diagnostic" to see how much the kids already knew about the content we'd be studying that year. I noticed that Petey had only written about three lines or so before putting his head down, pulling his hood up, and going to sleep. Even though we're not supposed to offer assistance during activities like this, I went over to Petey's desk, tapped on it twice with my nails, and simply whispered, "Hey. I *know* you can do more." I think he was just being polite because we were fairly new to each other and he might not have wanted to create an issue with me that early on. So he grudgingly picked up the No. 2 testing pencil he was using and continued to write. He proceeded to fill up the four provided test booklet pages, wait for my attention, point at the pages, shoot me a wide-toothed grin, and lay his head back down on the desk. I remember smiling wryly and saying to myself, *You win, you little bugger. But you haven't seen the last of me.*

There are countless stories like this about Petey, and similar stories about hundreds of other students I've encountered. It's amazing to see kids turn around. Over the last few years, Petey became one of those very special diamonds in the rough. I likened him to the process of gold panning. As the miners separate the gold from the surrounding gravel and sediment, the most precious part remains. I can just picture the gold glistening in the pan, as the rest of the muck falls to the wayside. Petey *is* that gold (and actually, his journals functioned as the muck that helped reveal his sparkle). This kid was just one of those that stuck with you: one whom you'd worry about over the weekend, or be so excited to see the look on his face when you returned an assignment with a giant sticker on it. (Sure, you'd get the "tough guy" act at first, but in a quiet moment, your eyes would connect with his and the expression exchanged needed no words—it was tacit. He appreciated you, and you were stacking up positive points in his life).

The changes started taking place in the first year after I had Petey—his sophomore year. At the start of that year, some nonsense had come down the pike from the State Department of Education. The state was requiring something called Student Achievement

Assessments (affectionately shortened to SAAs, pronounced "Sozz." Someone said they should flip it around and call it ASS, which most of my colleagues agreed with vehemently). Basically, we were being asked to create arbitrary tests for our kids for the sole purpose of proving that they showed growth over the year. Huh? (Didn't kids naturally show growth every year?). They wanted us to come up with at least two SAAs to give to students (although *three* were "strongly recommended"). I guess they were implemented to have actual "proof" that teachers were teaching something to the kids. But I thought that was a given…I mean, wasn't that a basic job requirement? We had supervisors and administrators to ensure that was happening, right? Could no one be trusted anymore?

So it started with basically making an extra four tests a year (in addition to any of your own tests given during the year). In this case, you had to give two at the beginning of the year and two at the end. The first two would show what the kids came in knowing; the second two would prove they learned something since the score was expected to be much higher than the first. You had to make sure the exams covered different material (so I guess if you were a history teacher, you could give one test on the fall of Rome and another test on the French Revolution).

Call me crazy, but didn't teachers already do this? It seemed like a redundancy and almost a "cover your butt" type of task (probably another reason teachers wanted to call this new process ASS, I suppose). As it was, our particular district already gave a "diagnostic" at the beginning of each year (as did many other districts), so the SAAs would be additional. I didn't really understand the purpose— nor did colleagues in my own school and others. To make things worse, the new requirement was way beyond just making four tests.

There was a *load* of additional paperwork involved. At the risk of boring the layman, just trust me when I say that you had to basically justify every single question you put on the test (with additional proof that the questions were "challenging" enough), explain in paragraph form how the test applied to your subject, reference a list of state and national requirements in detailed form, cite your complete teaching profile and history, compile all of the student tests, and complete spreadsheets of data to prove that the kids had "shown growth" and learned something. Now remember, all of that is multiplied by *two* since you had to complete two separate SAAs. Did I mention that there were 128 students on my roster that year—all of whose tests I would have to grade (in addition to my regular assignments), times *two*. There was no such thing as being paid overtime for the hundreds of extra hours we would all end up putting in to this new initiative which seemed so pointless. I started to wonder when I would actually get to start *teaching* the kids information instead of just testing them. Are *you* confused? We certainly were.

If you've ever known a teacher personally, you probably know that our time is limited. I'm not complaining about this—we accept it as fact going into this profession. But it is a truth about the job. If you become a teacher, every single minute of your day is accounted for. You are scheduled from the moment you walk in until the last bell. After the last bell, you work feverishly to get done everything that can't be done while you're *working* all day. Obviously, you can't get to your own tasks when kids are in front of you all day. I can't tell you how many times I've gone without eating for about twenty-two hours straight (I'm serious) because the day got away from me, or how I've had to hold in my poop because I had thirty teenagers in front of me and I'm not legally allowed to leave them unsupervised.

I wish I were exaggerating. (I also read somewhere that teachers have the highest number of urinary tract infections because they're constantly holding in their pee until they can get to the bathroom. It's actually quite comical to watch *dozens* of teachers race for any available bathroom at the end of the school day. I sometimes amuse myself by standing back and watching this phenomenon).

When I've had guest speakers from the corporate world come in to my classes, it never fails that before they leave, they comment on the "poor working conditions." It's hard not to laugh when they ask about running to the local convenience store for a coffee at lunch time. I have to sympathetically remind them that our "lunch hour" is only thirty minutes. The shocked looks on their faces are truly priceless. It's not their fault—they truly weren't aware beforehand that this is how it is. The same thing happens annually during "student-teacher switch day" at our school. Kids who take on the role of teacher sit down exhausted at the end of the day and ask, "you really have to do this much work *every* day? I had no idea it was like this. I'm never becoming a teacher." That's always good for a laugh. But it's really just the nature of the beast. We teachers all know this. And we accept it.

But how was I supposed to be a good teacher if this new requirement was being added on top of my regular workload? Teaching is a profession where the educators create work for themselves on a daily basis. It's self-governing. (Well, it used to be. We used to prepare lessons, teach them, and then assess the kids on what they learned. We did this stuff all day long. Those who hired us were getting a lot of services at a *bargain* rate for the zillion tasks we did daily. And we did them willingly—because it was all from the heart. It was all about the kids. It wasn't just a "job"). But I mean it in all seriousness when I say that it almost seemed as though the system didn't want us to teach or do what we had done before. It felt like we were all just supposed to be cookie-cutter robots that simply handed out tests and compiled data.

As I've said, it used to be that we could really reach kids and make a positive impact on them. But now we were being asked to take valuable time out of what was *important* to prove to the "powers-that-be" that kids were showing growth. I mentioned earlier that in my opinion, you can't teach kids anything until you have established rapport and relationships with them. The implementation of SAAs would inevitably take away from that precious time. The kids would no sooner enter your room at the start of the year and you would have to hand them two separate tests. That's a fine "how'd'ya do". If I were a kid, I'd be resistant, too. I'd probably even give the teacher a dirty look or make a nasty comment for greeting me that way.

Which brings me to my next point—what control did the teacher really have in making sure the kids would in fact show growth? I mean, a teacher could do a whole song and dance in front of the class and be the most interesting and entertaining showman in town, but that didn't mean every child was going to try to get something out of his or her class. What if the student slept through class the whole year? What if they didn't get along with the teacher and purposely didn't try? What if they were absent all the time because they had health issues? What if they had test anxiety? (I mean, honestly, how many of us would really want the arbiter of *our* worth and *our* "growth" to be whittled down to a single test score? Most of us would cringe at the idea of having to share what score we got on a college entrance exam or a state test). Not to mention the obvious *increase* in testing this created for all kids in all of their classes. If they were taking two of these in *every subject* they had, then a whole lot of testing was just added to their school year—and the coming years. (Important side note: for a long time, I have heard people scoff at how American students are falling behind the students in other countries; however, they fail to recognize that America is one of the few countries that attempts to educate *every* citizen. Other nations are highly selective about those who are formally educated. It's a "privilege" for only the most promising children. America chooses to educate *every* child. So of course if you have the very elite stacked up against the majority, the playing field isn't equal. In addition, maybe we should look in the mirror and see what some of our kids are faced with today. I have students who live in homeless shelters or motels. Their first concern might not be competing with kids in other nations).

And quite honestly, if I were a kid today, school tests would be last on my list. Our kids today have bigger fish to fry than we once did. I've mentioned the baggage they're coming in with. Who can stay focused if their parents' marriage is crumbling in front of them, or their grandmother just died? I've had students who have been diagnosed with intense anxiety and severe depression. (Some of them were even on medications that made them zombies in class). The list goes on and on. Again, these were *humans* we were talking about. They couldn't be quantified in numbers. One bad day could skew test scores, and we all have bad days. I'm not sure who I felt sorrier for—us, or the kids.

That said, the first day of Petey Guzman's sophomore year, I had piles of SAA paperwork sitting on my desk. We had been given our new marching orders just days before the school year began and the pressure was fresh upon all of us staff members. I can't tell you how awful I felt being so dismissive with Petey. It wasn't like me, and I knew he could tell. I prided myself on being genuine and authentic with my kids—but I clearly wasn't myself that day and he was able to sniff it out. (Most teens can).

I realized something the very moment Petey crossed the threshold of my classroom door that day and left with a forlorn look on his face, notebook in hand. Something happened. It was a single moment, yet incredibly poignant. It was then that I became all too familiar with the emotion we call *disappointment*: disappointment that my own life was going to become crunching numbers and creating data spreadsheets instead of *teaching*; disappointment that I would be letting down my kids who didn't recognize this new robotic test-giver; and disappointment my kids—especially Petey—would have in *me* as a result of these new changes.

# CHAPTER 5

I started to feel pretty good. The weeks were passing by pretty quickly sophomore year, which was kinda nice cuz so often the school year just *dragged on*. I was writing a lot. I'd find time to write in the morning before school, at the end of a class period if the teacher ended early, and sometimes—I even surprised myself with this—if I got to my next class early enough. I'd sit down real quick and hurriedly finish an entry or get started on a new one before the class began. I was writing at home quite a bit, too. Even though I could usually be found playing video games after school (especially my current favorite, *Demon Hunter VI*), lately I had been writing in my journal in the afternoons—sometimes right up until I went to bed. My mom seemed pleased. One night she popped her head into my bedroom and saw me propped up on my bed, blue pen scribbling furiously into my tattered notebook.

"Hey, you. Is this my son in here using a *pen* instead of some other weapon to slay demons right now?" She laughed and sat down next to me. I didn't respond right away cuz I was absorbed in what I was doing. "You writing to Ms. Moore?" There was a long pause of silence.

I finally looked up. "Hey, Ma. Yeah—sorry. I was just trying to finish up this entry. I was telling her about stupid math class with Old Man Schillings. He's *so* old, Ma."

She laughed. "Well, I would say I was worried about you, doing too much of one activity, but I'm thrilled it's writing that you're doing. You know how many parents can say their teenage son is *writing* and not doing something obnoxious or dangerous?" She side-hugged me and kissed my head.

"Don't tell anyone, Ma. I don't want people thinking I have no life."

"Your secret's safe with me," she said, her eyes narrowing at me as though she were holding some top-secret government information. She perked up. "You know, midyear evaluations were e-mailed to parents today. B's and C's I saw. Much better than last year, honey. I'd love to see you at A's and B's though." She winked at me and her lips formed a smile.

"Thanks, Ma. I actually think the writing's helping to keep me focused. It's like a little game with myself. I try to rush through my work so I can go back to writing."

"Well, don't rush *too* much. You don't wanna turn in sloppy work." She paused. "But if I had to choose between writing or video games as an after-homework activity, I'd take writing *any* day." She squeezed me again, and then stood up and headed for the door. Before heading out, she glanced back.

"Listen, I've got a shift at the store tonight. But Ricky will be home if you need anything."

"Greaaaat," I said, my voice dripping in sarcasm. "Maybe we can do some stepfather-son bonding."

My mom sighed. "I know you two don't get along, honey. And I know he won't ever replace your real dad."

"He *is* kind of an asshole, Ma. That's for sure."

"Peter Manuel Guzman," she admonished, eyes wide. "That kind of language is unacceptable in this household." It was interesting that she had used my full name. Why do parents always do that when they're pissed? Her accent came out more, too, when she was angry. Beyond that, though, I noticed the irony in her statement: *Manuel* had been my real father's first name. I started to feel the sting that comes when your eyes get ready to fill with tears. I couldn't help it—I really fucking missed him. I shook my head, pushing the thoughts away. *Get your shit together, man.*

"Sorry, Ma, but Dad would've agreed with me that Ricky's an ass—" I stopped myself. "A—not very nice person." I lowered my eyes. I actually really hated upsetting my mom. She'd always been really good to me, and I damn well knew it. I just didn't agree with her choice to be with this dude. That's really the only issue we'd ever had between us.

My mom took a deep breath—the kind where, like, it could've been called a sigh, but it was really just her own acknowledgement that it was a tense subject.

"You know, Ricky's also been saying how much he's noticed that you're playing video games a lot less."

That was her peace treaty. She wanted me to give in, which honestly was easier to do since she had done it first. She knew me well because that *totally* was my style. I mean, I was willing to apologize or admit I was wrong—but *only* if the other person threw me a bone first. Otherwise, I'd fight to the death. (The demons in my game could vouch for me on this). I had to say, though, she had a point. Ricky and I *had* been arguing a lot less—probably because I was spending more time writing to Ms. Moore than playing video games—which had always been a huge source of my arguments with him. (Geez, Ms. Moore was even helping me improve stepfather relations. Damn, she was good). I conceded.

"That's great, Ma. And thanks for letting me know you're working late. I'll try to raise some of my grades, too—just for you."

"Don't *try*—just *do*." One of her famous sayings. She smiled, and then proceeded out the door.

It *was* pretty cool that I had been doing better in school that year. I gotta tell ya, people hassled you a lot less if you just got with the program and did what was asked of you. It was like they had a lot less to bitch about if you were on track—like you weren't giving them any ammo to use against you. Not that B's and C's were all that great. But for me, it was a pretty big improvement compared to the D's and F's I'd gotten the previous year—well, except for the *A* I had maintained in Ms. Moore's all year.

And speaking of, she had been doing a good job keeping up with my journals even though they were getting kinda longer and longer. I was covering the usual topics: girls, sports, my grades, math class. She was getting my notebook back to me within a week or so, sometimes less. And her comments were still copious (a new vocab word I learned in English this year. Ms. Moore was also responsible for making me like vocabulary instruction). It seemed that she had either settled into her year or gotten used to the workload. I had even mentioned in one of my entries to her that I was worried about her availability this year since she had been acting so weird in the beginning. But it seemed like she had proven me wrong. She appeared present, available, and fully armed with her pink pen. Then again, people say the eye of the storm comes just before that shit's gonna blow right up in your face.

# CHAPTER 6

By the time midyear evaluations had rolled around, it finally felt like there was some semblance of teaching going on. At that point, SAAs had been given, data had been compiled, and it seemed logical that we might have to actually give some instruction before the end-of-year SAAs could be given (the ones which would determine whether the kids learned something or not). Don't get me wrong—those months of the SAA planning and implementation—they were awful. I could barely keep up with my day-to-day lessons (if you could even call them that. Test-giving and test-prepping was more like it). Any teacher you saw around the building looked completely defeated. I saw teachers turning gray before my very eyes. You know those pictures they show of a President—before and after their term? Well, teachers around our building and all throughout the state looked the same way, except the "term" had been condensed into a couple of months. I saw teachers who weren't ready to retire yet put in for early retirement. I could hear them muttering, "This isn't teaching. It isn't fun anymore. I don't even have *time* to teach my kids." It was incredibly discouraging. Everywhere you looked, teachers were burned out, frustrated, angry, ready to resign, or about to break down crying. (I witnessed all five of those that year—more than once for each). I mean, truly, across the state, you could meet someone new, find out they were a teacher, and then ask them how their SAAs were going; no kidding, the return look they'd give would have made an outsider think you had asked them how the treatment of their terminal illness was going. It was like an epidemic. Teachers across the state were mostly depressed, dissatisfied with their jobs, and looking to make major career changes. A dear friend of mine from college is a clinical psychologist and has her own private practice for marriage and family therapy. She told me that the number of teachers who signed up for individual counseling that year was through the roof. She and other therapist colleagues had such a high influx of teachers once the SAAs were implemented, they almost couldn't keep up with the number of new clients. They had to extend their hours, take on weekend shifts, and provide sliding scale fees (since everyone knows teacher salaries are just pitiful).

Luckily for me, when it came to Petey and other students of mine who were submitting journals, I happened to get a break. Nothing too crazy was going on in my students' lives. They were writing about normal "teen-angst" type stuff. They wanted advice on their boyfriends, or prom dates, or annoying little sisters. They referenced pro basketball players and the newest video game that was out (some nonsense called *Demon Hunter VI.* That was a fun part of teaching, watching the cycles of things kids found to be "in" or "out." I couldn't believe *Demon Hunter* was *still* on the up and up. It certainly had a strong following). Those kinds of journals were easy to get through in terms of offering feedback. I could buzz through those, offer lots of notes, and the kids were happy.

That was usually the way of it. Student journals would ebb and flow. It always seemed that either a lot was going on, or all was quiet. And I loved having that ongoing discourse with them. It kept me in the loop with things. It allowed me an inside look into what was going on in students' lives and what was important to them. It helped explain why a kid may have been moody one day, or why they were so giddy on a Friday afternoon (in that case, her Sweet Sixteen birthday was the next day).

The problem, of course, would come when kids wrote about intense topics. As I mentioned, a lot of these kids were dealing with major baggage. I'm not sure if I explained this part to you yet... Teachers are "mandated reporters" so if a kid happens to write or say something that could indicate some sort of harm to their well-being or another's, we are mandated by law to report it. You can imagine the can of worms this opens for teachers like me. English teachers in general have a high frequency of this happening, simply because our assignments include so much student writing. But teachers like me are even more susceptible to it because I actually *invite* kids to write to me about their personal lives all year. (I know, I know—stupid, right? It's like I'm asking for it. I should just assign dittos or questions in the textbook or something to avoid having to deal with all the personal stuff. And I'm sure some teachers do. But I'm in the business of *kids*—and that means all that goes with it. Not just my subject material. Plus, I want them to have a safe outlet. I want them to have a therapeutic way to express themselves. And honestly, I'd rather look myself in the mirror every day knowing I reported a kid who was being abused which resulted in them getting life-saving help, than just turning a blind eye to what these kids are facing). Sorry—tangent. I'm working on limiting those.

If it so happened that a student wrote something which legally required reporting, a whole process would ensue. First, we would have to show evidence of what the child shared, then the Guidance Department would get involved. Sometimes we'd have to sit in on meetings, documentation would be a must (more paperwork—yay!), and then some sort of action plan would go into place. Perhaps Child Protective Services would get involved, or a student might be put into counseling (or hospitalized, or drug rehab—whatever the situation called for). I'm sure you could also imagine how this would suck up an entire work day. Forget about running off copies on your prep period or taking a poop in between classes. You'd be spending any second that wasn't in front of a classroom of kids doing this paperwork, attending the meetings, reporting what you knew, etc. And again—I didn't mind doing it—ever. The whole purpose was to make sure the kids were safe and ok. The problem would naturally come when there would cease to be time for that kind of stuff. (After all, SAAs and "student growth" were way more important than a kid's well-being, right?).

Because I had been so bogged down by SAAs for the first few months of the year, I thought my journal writing back to kids would have suffered. Fortunately, though, the new policy came during a time when most kids weren't writing about dangerous topics that required reporting. Even Petey's were pretty tame for the time being.

If I had a stack of student journals to read, I always put Petey's aside for last. He had such a strong voice in his writing—it was sheer entertainment. After a long day, his entries could always make me smile. I loved reading his cynical views on teenage life. Because his entries had been pretty surface-level during these months, my amount of pink ink was consistent with my usual. I was pretty proud of myself for juggling my usual workload with the added stress of the SAAs. I felt like super-teacher. Maybe I *could* do it all. I could handle whatever they kept throwing at us on top of the usual workload. I could keep going at this level without ever getting burned out, right? Of course. Sure.

Then came the Michaels Model for Teacher Evaluation.

# CHAPTER 7

Her name was Kelsey. And she was just about the cutest thing you ever saw in sixth period science class. Forget those frogs and other shit you dissected—Kelsey was seriously the cutest specimen in the room. (Wow, I think I just made a joke. Maybe this journal writing really *was* making me a better writer. I wasn't as "stoic" as Ms. Moore originally said I was freshman year. I may have actually started to develop a sense of humor). Now normally, I would be into girls that were curvier (I mean, my Puerto-Rican heritage could've told you that). But this girl was actually teensy-weensy. (I could just hear my mom saying, "She's cute as a button!"). And she was. She was about the same size, too. Kelsey was this tiny little blond girl with freckles who sat in front of me. Her last name was Gibraldi, so naturally she had the desk in front of me since teachers always sat kids in alphabetical order. (I never understood why they did that... They always said it was so that they could learn names, but I think it was just so it spaced out guys and girls evenly in an effort to minimize chit-chat. I mean, really—no teacher was trying to memorize the *last* names of kids, anyway. For the record, Ms. Moore never did that. She didn't micro-manage us. We were allowed to sit wherever we wanted, so long as it didn't cause a problem. I liked that she treated us more like adults. It was on us to keep the privilege.

And really no one abused it. She kinda gave us the chance to begin with, and we respected it and were able to keep it).

I had started to write about her in my journal to Ms. Moore. I kinda needed advice. To be honest, I'm not super-smooth with the ladies. I hate guys who come off all suave and charming. Those are the kind of guys that remind me of Ricky—and that was the *last* thing I wanted to be like. Plus, I think most girls can see right through it. They know when a guy is just trying to get in their pants. (I'm gonna be honest, and you're probably gonna think I'm lame, but I'm still a virgin. My mom always told me it was best to wait for someone special, and if there's one thing she demanded, it was to respect women. She said that my dad had *always* respected her, and that it was the right thing for men to hold women up high. I liked that. I always thought it was a classy way to view that kind of stuff… which was another reason I could never understand why my mom was with Ricky. Something about his urbane nature just rang false. I don't know. I guess my mom fell for it. Ha!—*urbane*: another new vocab word).

One thing I didn't really like to ever see was girls cry. That drove me nuts. There was one day in science class that we got our unit tests back, and Kelsey had gotten a *C* on hers. Even though she sat in front of me, I could tell by the way she was slumped over her desk that she must not have gotten a good grade. I had gotten a *D* on mine (no surprise there), so I was just happy I passed. But it was known that Kelsey was a straight-A student, so it was a little out of character for her to have done anything less than perfect.

"Hey, Kels," I whispered, tapping her on the shoulder. "You ok?" She turned around and that was when I saw her teensy blue eyes brimming with tears.

"Not really," she whispered back. "I got a *C*. I can't believe it. I studied and everything."

"Well, hey, I got a *D*, so I'll help ya study for the next test," I said smiling. To that, she giggled, which was super-cute cuz her whole face kinda collapsed when she did. I was about to ask her about maybe hanging out when this scummy kid, Josh, came over and sat down on top of Kelsey's desk.

"Hey, Kelsey, you coming to the basketball game tonight? You know I'm starting."

She kind of recoiled the way a snake would, and the smile left her face.

"Well, Josh, I *am* a cheerleader, so I'll probably be there whether you're starting or not."

I couldn't help but smile. He looked kind of confused, like he couldn't tell whether she was insulting him or worshipping him. He nodded and sauntered off two rows over back to his own desk. She turned to me and rolled her eyes.

"I mean, did he even see that I was upset? He's so into himself." We were interrupted by the sound of Mrs. Paterson's voice, wanting to go over the test. As far as I was concerned, the score was 2-0 between me and Josh, with me in the lead.

Josh was just the type of kid I was talking about who pissed me off. Yeah, he was a star athlete and yeah, he was pretty smooth with the ladies. He was the kinda kid who also tried to be a class clown and teacher's pet, but I honestly think he annoyed most teachers. It was like his jokes fell flat. Ms. Moore was great at squashing that kinda shit. She could always tell when kids were genuine and when they were douche bags. I appreciated that about her. She was real discerning about that stuff. I didn't have Josh in any of my classes until this year, which was good cuz I found him seriously annoying. He was also the type of kid who picked on the little guy. I hate that shit. He was super-arrogant and really thought he was God's gift to everyone. The fact that he had to pick on guys who maybe were scrawnier than he was or nerdier than he was just proved how insecure he was. Pissed me off.

I had been writing to Ms. Moore about the science class happenings, and I gotta say, while she would still get my journal back to me within a week's time as usual, I had noticed that her notes were a little thin. I mean, usually my pages were covered in pink. Lately, her replies had been a little sparse. It was almost like she was rushing to get it back in time and was just skimming what I had written to put in minor comments here and there. I felt a little uneasy about it, but I tried to just shrug it off. Maybe she had just been busy for this batch of entries. She'd probably get back to the tons of feedback I was used to getting the next time I submitted. Yeah, definitely.

# CHAPTER 8

During our February staff meeting, we were informed that additional measures from the state were being put in place to evaluate teacher performance. Even though SAAs had been implemented, the State Department of Education felt those weren't enough. Since it was a brand new calendar year, they wanted teachers to be rated in yet another way. Every school in the state had to adopt a model with a point system in order to rank and rate teachers. Our building leaders chose an evaluation model entitled, the "Michaels Model for Teacher Evaluation." Basically, before the school year was over, someone would come into our classroom three separate times to observe whatever lesson was going on. Then, they would rate us with points to let us know whether we were considered "unsatisfactory," "basic," "proficient," or "advanced." Observations were nothing new—we were used to having building administrators stop in to see lessons and sometimes even participate. Usually, it was a collegial, collaborative, welcoming, reciprocal experience. With this new system though, it pitted administrators against teachers to fight for points. It also pitted teachers against other teachers in terms of who scored higher or lower than another colleague. The whole thing left most of us just shaking our heads. Almost immediately, I could sense its impact of making teachers strive for mediocrity instead of excellence. Whereas most of us had always taken great pride in our work, striving for perfection (even if that wasn't plausible when working with humans), now it seemed that people felt so swamped, they would just try to keep from drowning and get by. They would shoot to achieve "basics" or "proficients" instead of "advanced" because the pressure was just too great. They didn't feel encouraged; they felt beaten down again. No one could be perfect all the time. That just wasn't the nature of teaching. It was more of an art—not a science. And so many different factors went into a single lesson. There were so many variables in a given classroom, and again, we weren't scientists who were controlling these variables for an experiment. God forbid a teacher received too many "basics" or "unsatisfactorys." If that happened, you'd be put on probation and potentially lose your job if you didn't raise your score. The funny part was, it was meant to make the system fair and objective—except it was purely *subjective*. You would be rated by a single person's rating and opinion each and every time.

Different districts chose different models. Interestingly, our school chose the one invented by Doug Michaels, an entrepreneur from the corporate world who had no previous or current experience in education. He was simply a sales executive who had invented a rating system for products in his inventory. It was later adapted to the teaching world. I couldn't help but laugh realizing that they were trying to use a rating system initially intended for inanimate objects to now quantify humans and human performance. (Maybe we really were just "products"). It seemed like one big financial scheme, too— the more schools that adopted the model, the more Mr. Michaels would cash in (as would other teacher evaluation inventors). There was money to be made in the software for the program, training manuals, workshops, and "experts" who would come in to schools to "train" us on how to achieve the highest ratings possible. Again, it just felt like another thing on our list to help try and prove that we deserved to have (or maintain) our current job positions. (Although at this point, who would even *want* this career?).

I don't think most of us would've cared so much, except that this meant more paperwork (yet again), and more time and energy spent on this instead of the kids in our classrooms. With this model (as with most, I came to find out), teachers would get observed a minimum of three times (with a separate rating for each), and be required to attend pre- and post- meetings for each observation. In those, we would be required to present lesson plans, activities, materials, student rosters, student testing data (such as standardized test scores), student profiles of medical issues, behavioral issues, etc. Even though these were things we normally had in our brains during every lesson, this was outside additional work that had to be painstakingly documented (in writing) to ensure you met several different areas on the rating system for a single lesson. Honestly, it would be long and tedious to explain all the ins and outs of this in detail, but trust me when I tell you it most definitely resulted in taking more time out of your kids and classroom, and putting more into logistics and showcasing a "dog-and-pony-show" to prove you were doing meaningful things in your classroom (which we were already doing every day).

At the time of the new marching orders, I fell a little behind in my journal responses to students. I was ashamed to admit that I basically had to skim kids' entries, and put a bare minimum of comments on them in return. I had already been contacted by one of my vice principals informing me that I would get observed early March, so I had been preparing for our first pre-observation meeting.

The paperwork felt endless and sucked up countless hours each day for me. (After all, since you knew that your whole year of teaching was dependent on only three lessons they would randomly come in to see, you had to bring your "A-game" and make sure each lesson was virtually flawless). I felt annoyed and resentful that my students' journals were having to be put on the back burner once again for these new initiatives. This had already happened before during SAAs, and now it was happening again. Would I ever again be able to focus on reaching my kids and making a difference? That was the whole reason I originally went into this profession. I scoured the rating system to see where that fell in terms of points. Interesting. "Investing time and energy in kids' lives" was nowhere on the list.

# CHAPTER 9

Ok, so I got suspended for fighting. But I didn't throw the first punch…well, actually, that's not true. I did. But Josh started it. I was only responding to what he began. A week or two after the science test that Kelsey got a *C* on, and I got a *D* on, we were in class toward the end of the period, taking notes on some new chapter information. We finished about three minutes before the bell, so everyone was just putting away their notebooks and talking. That's when I overheard Josh giving some freshman kid a hard time. Even though it was a sophomore class, this kid must've been pretty smart because he was trying to "double-up" his science courses his freshman year to try and take some more advanced ones the following year. He was kinda a small kid, probably only a buck ten soaking wet, but Josh just wouldn't let up. He was taunting the kid for being nerdy and being younger in a sophomore class. Like I said, that kind of shit really got under my skin. We had actually spent some time in Ms. Moore's class last year on the topic of bullying, and how really anyone who stands by and lets it happen is basically as bad as the bully. I could see the freshman kid's face getting all red and embarrassed, and I couldn't stand to witness any more of it.

"Yo, Josh, why don't you shut the fuck up? Leave him alone."

"What did you say to me?" He turned away from the kid and turned to face me.

"You heard me. Lay off it."

"And who are you—his bodyguard? Oh, wait. You're his *gay* lover. I always knew you were a fucking faggot."

Wrong thing to say to me. I was ready to fuck this kid up.

"Say it again, motherfucker."

"All right, you fucking homo. Faggot." That time when he said it, he actually pushed me backward, putting both hands on my upper chest. That's when I swung. (I had a nice right cross—one of the tactics I used repeatedly in *Demon Hunter*, too).

It wasn't long before we were wrestling around on the classroom floor, and Mrs. Paterson had run into the hallway to grab one of the security officers. Big Al, one of the guards who used to work in the middle school but moved up with us to the high school, rushed in and pulled me off of Josh.

"Ok, Petey, enough! It's not worth it." He had known me personally from my middle school days. I liked him and actually respected him. He was a retired state trooper who had known my dad back in the day. They had sometimes worked together at the Port Authority. He was really only working security in our building to keep busy during retirement.

At the same time Big Al got to me, a different guard grabbed Josh and started to cart him off toward the nurse's office. He was bleeding a bit. I couldn't help but feel a bit smug about that. I caught eyes with Kelsey as I was being escorted out. She smiled at me with a little bit of admiration I thought. I smiled back. Not gonna lie, I felt like I had won again. Petey: 4, Josh: still 0.

Big Al walked me to the main office to be "processed." I knew the fight probably meant suspension. At our school, getting suspended was pretty much a given for fighting. I figured my mom would be disappointed in me, but I couldn't help it—Josh was being such a dick to the freshman kid. Maybe mom would be proud I had stood up for the kid. I knew I would have to explain myself to her later. But right now, the one person I wanted to talk to was Ms. Moore. I was still pretty heated and I knew she would know the right thing to say. Besides mom, she was probably the only other person on the planet who would've been able to calm me down. She was right in the building too, so she'd be quicker access than my mother.

"Hey, Al, do you know if Ms. Moore's around? I'd feel better if I could speak to her."

"Let me check with one of the secretaries," he replied in his usual gruff voice.

I sat down in one of the main office chairs. My right hand hurt a bit, but it was no big deal. I knew that they usually tried to send one kid to the nurse and the other to the main office so that there was a separated "cool-off" period and the kids involved wouldn't have to face each other for a bit. I smiled inwardly, knowing they had taken Josh to the nurse first. (It was usual protocol for the kid who was hurt worse to be brought to the nurse first. That was victory in itself to be the kid sent to the office first. Josh was such a pussy. It felt good slugging him).

I was pretty sure Ms. Moore had an off period at that point during the day, so I expected that she would be available to talk and listen to what had happened. Maybe she could even vouch for me that I was a mostly decent kid. One of the secretaries came over to me while I was seated and explained that Ms. Moore was in a meeting and would "probably be a while." I sighed. What else was new? It felt like she was never available anymore when I needed her. I knew it probably wasn't her fault, but I almost started to wonder whether it was an excuse. Like maybe they had called her classroom, and she didn't feel like dealing with me, so she told them to tell me she "had a meeting" and "was busy." I wasn't trying to be needy or demanding, but recently, it felt like Ms. Moore wasn't all there. And since suspension was probably inevitable, I guessed I wouldn't be seeing her for seven to nine days or so. Seriously, would she even notice if I was gone?

# CHAPTER 10

The day of my first observation on the Michaels Model had arrived. Luckily, it was scheduled for first period, so at least I could get it out of the way. On the other hand, it was possible that kids could still be half-asleep at the 7:26 start time, so I'd have to hope they had all slept well the night before (instead of honing their skills for *Demon Hunter*), eaten hearty breakfasts, and gotten hugs and "I love yous" from two adoring parents prior to arriving. Wishful thinking, I supposed. During homeroom, I tried to make sure every last component of the lesson was set up and ready to go. I had tested my projector earlier that morning (because Lord knows technology failed sometimes), rearranged all the desks into a unique formation conducive to the lesson, and counted all photocopies a second time to make sure I had more than enough. It was necessary to pull out all the stops if I had any hope of getting an evaluation that wouldn't put the job I loved at risk. Hopefully, it would go well. While I was taking the attendance of my homeroom students, I overheard two boys jabbering excitedly, but in hushed tones.

"Yeah, he laid him out. Josh was bleeding everywhere. It was awesome."

"Good, I'm glad Petey kicked his ass. That Josh kid's a total dick."

I smiled at the two boys, then gently reminded, "Gentlemen, I'm getting old. My ears begin to bleed when I hear that kind of language. Can we try to use respectful language around our elders?" The boys both lowered their heads, sheepish expressions creeping on to their faces. One of them spoke up.

"Sorry, Ms. Moore. We didn't think you could hear us."

I laughed. "Wow, elderly *and* hard of hearing, huh? Maybe I *should* retire sooner than later!" I started to resume scanning the room for attendance and then felt my stomach drop.

"Wait a minute, guys. Did you say Petey?" The same boy who had spoken up before nodded his head.

"Yeah. You should've seen it, Ms. Moore. Petey Guzman, like, kicked this kid's *ass*. Oops. Sorry—I meant butt. He got suspended for like five days cuz the office found out the other kid's the one who technically started it. The Josh kid's out for like nine days, I think."

*Oh, no.* All of a sudden, I felt like I might vomit.

"Were they ok? Was anyone hurt?"

"Nah, I heard they're both fine. But Josh got nurse duty first. Petey definitely won the fight." He saw my eyes narrow at him. "Not that winning a fight matters," he quickly added.

The bell rang, signaling the end of homeroom. The boys made a swift exit, barreling for the door. I sat down for a moment. All of these thoughts came rushing to my mind. *Was Petey really ok? What had happened? What started the fight? He hadn't mentioned anything in his journal...or had he? Had I missed something? How could I not have known about this? How did I not even know he had been suspended? Was I slipping? And when was he returning to school? Oh, my gosh, I hope he's ok.*

Kids had started pouring in for first period. No time to agonize over Petey. I was about to be observed even though I felt like running to the bathroom to vomit, or running to the main office to find out if Petey was ok. Wonderful. My mind was elsewhere. This was sure to be a great lesson.

# CHAPTER 11

Most kids probably would've liked being suspended. (I've even heard people call it a "paid vacation"). But I really didn't. I mean, I loved *Demon Hunter* and all, but there was only so much I could play of it before even I had enough. (I don't know—I almost appreciated that game more when I had to fit it in to my schedule than when I just had access to it all day every day). Plus, being suspended meant I was losing valuable time with Kelsey. Someone else in class could've been getting closer to her. (Well, at least I could be sure that person wasn't Josh!). It also was gonna suck getting back and having to do all that make-up work. Let's face it—I probably wouldn't do it anyway and then I'd *really* be in danger of failing classes for the marking period. Maybe Kelsey could help me get caught up.

My mom had actually been pretty supportive about the whole thing. She was upset when she first heard. But after hearing the details, she was proud I had stood up for the freshman kid. Ricardo of course gave me some lip about what an idiot I was for getting suspended. That was probably the worst part of suspension—being home with him more than usual. At least mom was on my side. I wasn't too concerned with what asshole Ricky thought of me. I ignored him most of the time, and got my thoughts out in my journal.

I couldn't wait to drop off this set of entries to Ms. Moore. This collection was *full* of interesting shit. She'd probably really enjoy it. And I'd probably get a lot of pink notes in return.

On my first day back after suspension, mom had to go with me to be readmitted. That was part of the drill. Anytime a kid got suspended, you usually had to meet with the principal before resuming classes. The meeting had been scheduled for 10am, which was kinda nice because that meant the first class I'd be going back to was lunch. I figured on my way, I'd stop by and see Ms. Moore, drop off my journal, and start to tell her what had happened. I wondered if she even knew anything about it.

I walked to her classroom, but when I got there, it was empty. The door was locked and the lights were out. I headed back to the main office to ask if she was absent today.

"No, she's here today, but she's behind closed doors right now." I paused, looking at the secretary, confused. "She's in a meeting, hon."

"Oh, um, ok. Can I like, leave her a message or something?"

"Not really. Maybe try e-mailing her?"

I walked back to the cafeteria feeling somewhere between sad and annoyed. Geez. Was it that much to ask to get to talk to my favorite teacher? Was Ms. Moore ever *not* in a meeting anymore? Did she still care about us? Did she even know about the fight? I mean, if she had heard about the fight, I didn't want her to think it was my fault. I didn't want her to think less of me. I wanted her to know the truth. I wanted her to know that I had stopped the bullying when I saw it—I was part of the *solution*, not the problem—just like we had discussed in her class. If I ever got to drop off my damn journal, she'd get to see my side. And she'd be proud. At least, I thought she would be. Maybe. If I ever got the chance to see her one of these days.

# CHAPTER 12

I wish I could say that my lesson had been amazing... That my post-observation meeting had gone beautifully... That my ratings were all "advanced" and that the narrative section where the observer writes lengthy comments about the lesson had been outstanding. But none of that would be true. Let's just say that after I left the post-meeting, I went back to my classroom and cried. I mean, really *cried*. I sat in the back of the room where no one could see me, with the lights off and the door locked. And actually, I had to get it together pretty fast because I had a class coming in four minutes after I arrived back at my room. I wiped my face and checked the mirror in my purse for bloodshot eyes. (The last thing I needed was someone reporting that I was using drugs. Although at least if that happened, I'd feel like that was something that earned being fired).

I buried my emotions, taught the remainder of the classes I had for the day, and after the last bell rang, I went back to the same corner of the classroom (lights off, door locked), and continued the crying I hadn't gotten to finish earlier. To say that the post-observation meeting had gone terribly was an understatement. I mean, I'm pretty hard on myself as a teacher, and I'm definitely my own worst critic, but I'm not exaggerating for effect here. I was completely depressed when I left that office.

Larry Pelts, a vice principal, had been my observer. "Lazy Larry" as he was known around our building, had been a gym teacher during his short career as an educator (four years, I believe). I've known gym teachers who put their heart and soul into their careers—some, whose time in education spanned decades. But Larry fit practically every stereotype you could think of when it came to gym teachers who did the bare minimum. The truth was, his heart was never in the instruction or the students themselves. He had always hoped to climb the ladder of administration. Yet once he had settled in to his VP position, he had stayed there. For the most part, I had always gotten along just fine with him—until he became my evaluator. Until he became the arbiter of my worth as a teacher.

He started the meeting by giving me his written report. There were some comments that I found disturbing. He said that during the lesson, at times I seemed to "lack focus" and had "less enthusiasm" than I usually exhibited. (Gee, could any of that have been a result of worrying about Petey?). He felt that I needed to "increase the rigor" in my class. (I had told him ahead of time that this class was my lowest-achieving group—had he forgotten that? For that particular group of kids, what I had been doing with them was already considered challenging). His comments (and my rebuttals) could go on forever. It was already devastating to me that this had all been put in writing. That meant it was on the record. And teachers really had no recourse. You honestly had to just sit there and take it.

Larry also noted that there was a semi-circle table in the room that I hadn't utilized. He mentioned that I had been "wasteful" with my resources. That was pretty funny. The lesson didn't even call for the use of that table. (I wondered if that part had to do with the fact that the district had just purchased those at the end of last year... maybe it was a money thing). It felt like a cruel joke that Larry's last name was "Pelts," considering the guy had in fact just "pelted" me with every negative remark possible—all of which were his opinion. So much for objectivity.

"One thing I also noticed," he said a bit condescendingly, "was that there were a lot of A's and B's in your gradebook. You really should be giving more C's and D's." He paused. "Oh! And I'd like to see more tests in there for each marking period."

I almost slid off my chair. He wanted me to give lower grades even if they weren't warranted? How was that ethical? Was there any integrity in grades anymore? And why had he been going through my gradebook? I mean, we were required to keep a computer gradebook nowadays, and we knew that supervisors had access to them, but typically there was a sense of professional courtesy with that type of thing. They didn't "check" on you. And he wanted more *tests*? That was downright humorous coming from a former gym teacher who had never been required to give tests. (I'm sure I don't even have to reiterate the lunacy of a guy with a physical education degree evaluating an English teacher: we weren't even in the same content area, so how could he even know what to look for in an English lesson?). With the recent implementation of SAAs, most parents were already complaining about the number of tests teachers were giving students, since they were in addition to regular class tests. Who was even my boss anymore? Whom was I supposed to be pleasing? Parents? Administrators? Government policymakers? (Did kids even factor in to the equation anymore?).

The resounding word in my head was *violated.* I just felt completely violated. Not only because Larry had gone through my gradebook (which made me long for the days of the paper gradebook which so many teachers had kept clutched to their chests), but also because it felt as though I was just being reduced to a lousy number. There was no longer any human element. It wasn't about reaching the kids. None of that seemed to matter. Pretty soon they would be telling us how many homework assignments we were allowed to give, and if we gave out too many stickers, or if too many kids were sneezing in class. Nefarious dictators from world history started to appear in my mind... I tried to push the thoughts away. That wasn't what was happening in education, was it?

Then I started to wonder if they were trying to get rid of me. It made sense. I *had* been there for the last twenty-two years, so naturally I was a little higher on the pay scale than teachers who were in their earlier years. Maybe they aimed to get me on the probation list—or even better, make me frustrated or disgusted enough that I'd leave on my own. (Then they could easily claim that it had nothing to do with them—that I had completely left on my own volition). I tried to squash the paranoia that was overwhelming me, but that was difficult. I had *never* before gotten a bad evaluation. I knew that maybe this hadn't been my best lesson, but I honestly had been anxious about the Petey situation and hadn't quite felt like myself. I still felt that it had gone pretty well, and the kids had been receptive, positive, and engaged. I mean, humans were sometimes affected by things. Was I allowed to be human anymore?

Larry ended up giving me three "basics" and one "proficient." There were points assigned to each, but they wouldn't all be averaged together until all three observations had taken place. I felt so completely dejected and defeated. I certainly didn't feel confident that I could do better on the next two observations. At that point, I figured they should probably just add my name to the probation list. I couldn't help but replay the whole meeting in my head again and again. I certainly wouldn't be sleeping well for the next few weeks.

I heard a knock at my classroom door which startled me so much I actually jumped a bit out of the student desk I'd been sitting in. I really didn't want to answer the door, but I had spent about two hours after school obsessing, so I figured it was time to face humanity again. A young woman, Patty, appeared at my door, looking somewhat grief-stricken herself. She had only been teaching about six years, and I had served as her mentor in her first year here.

"You're not gonna believe this. I just got out of a meeting with Ellen. Look at what she wrote on my post-observation report!" She thrust it into my hands. Ellen was another one of the vice principals.

Yikes. I thought *my* observation was bad. Patty had gotten all "basics" and even one "unsatisfactory." Maybe they were trying to get rid of young teachers, too.

"And do you know what she *said* to me?" she almost yelled, her face bright red. "She said that they were *told* that they're supposed to give us lower marks—even if we don't deserve them."

She went on to tell me that there were specific comments listed under the "student behavior" category that had also been unfavorable. Interestingly, even though her kids had been extremely well-behaved during her lesson, she didn't receive good marks because something in the Michaels Model deemed "optimum behavior" as some students misbehaving and other students *correcting* their behavior. Since all of her kids, however, had virtually been angels, higher marks couldn't be justified. (At that moment, I couldn't help but remember that the original Michaels Model had been for the *product* industry. In that case, it made sense that *improved* products would've received higher ratings than all basically decent. But now we were applying this to teenaged kids. It seemed ludicrous).

"Isn't that *crazy?*" she barked. "I mean, so it would've been better for the kids to be total jerks calling each other out for being jerks than if they were just all behaving appropriately? This is such crap. I don't even know why I went into this career. All I wanted to do was make a difference and help kids." Her voice started to crack, and then tears spilled down her face.

I honestly didn't even know what to say. Here I was, supposedly a "veteran" teacher, and I couldn't think of one thing to comfort her because her feelings echoed every single one of my own. Patty was one of the most vivacious, loving, golden-hearted teachers in our building. If they had *her* this upset, something was terribly wrong.

I stayed with her another hour before she finally left and I packed up for the day. It was so late I was afraid my husband would start calling the local hospitals to see if I had been admitted. (At that point, I almost felt like checking *myself* in). This would certainly make for some interesting dinner conversation tonight. Then again, why should he have to come home to a sad, miserable wife who was questioning everything about her job? It didn't seem fair to let Larry Pelts ruin my day, that night, or the next several weeks of my life. That wasn't logical. But it *was* personal. And the truth was, this job had always been *extremely* personal to me—to most of us. Wasn't that kind of the point?

I wanted to do something. I wanted to fight back. I wanted to be like those demon hunters in that silly video game, conquering the evil, fighting for good. But I didn't feel strong. I was beyond discouraged. I felt like giving up. I felt like looking for a different career.

# CHAPTER 13

After spring break, the school year seemed to fly by. You know how sometimes when you're asleep at night, you have those dreams where you're falling? It's like the earth is sliding out from underneath you? That's how the pace of the end of the year felt. It seemed like there were so many changes with everything happening so quickly. Let me start with Kelsey.

She ended up moving away in April. Totally sucked. Her dad worked for some big company and got transferred to somewhere in Colorado, so the whole family had to move. It was like one day she was here, and then she was gone. She only told me like two class periods before, and then she just wasn't in school again. So much for that. I mean, we probably could've done the whole, "let's stay in touch over e-mail and texting and stuff," but honestly, I'm smarter than that. I knew there was no chance in hell I'd really ever see her again, so what was the point? (At least I wouldn't have to compete with Josh over her, I guess).

Which, by the way, science class was going fine. Josh and I just kinda kept our distance after the fight, and we acted as if the other one didn't exist. Worked for me. He got busy with all of his jock stuff anyway, so we really had no interaction whatsoever. The whole thing just seemed to blow over.

Overall, I was doing mostly ok with classes. Some C's, a D or two, and a few B's. (Mom was happy about those). Some make-up work from the suspension got done, some didn't. (I figured I'd blamed Kelsey—if she had stayed here to help me, I'd probably be all caught up).

I did go to see Ms. Moore a couple times after the fight. Sometimes I went to drop off my journal, and other times I just went to talk. I don't know what had happened to Ms. Moore, but she just wasn't *right*. She seemed, like, I don't know—*depressed*. Every time I saw her, she had this sadness about her. One time I heard someone use the expression about a person "smiling through the tears," and that's exactly what Ms. Moore seemed like. I mean, don't get me wrong—I never saw her *crying* or anything, but she just didn't seem like herself. She wasn't really all there. I would go in and tell her stories and stuff, and it seemed like she was only half-listening. She was always hunched over her desk, surrounded by masses of paperwork. I never saw her fluttering about the room like she used to. She wasn't smiley and hyper like she had always been. It was just *weird*. She honestly looked miserable every time she was in her classroom—that is, when she was *in* her classroom.

I can't tell you how many times I went to see her and she wasn't there (at times that she should have been or usually was). When I *would* see her outside of her room, it always seemed like other teachers were whispering to her, or an administrator was talking to her, or she was in another "meeting." Did she ever teach anymore?

I didn't want to give up on her, but it seemed like she really couldn't be counted on. I still wanted to go to her, write to her, and confide in her and stuff, but it just seemed like I could never get 100% of her anymore. I wondered if other kids felt that way, too. Was she responding to other kids' journals? Did she have time for other students? Maybe she was just sick of me and all of my stupid issues. It was sad though. I felt like she was slipping away.

Our school year was scheduled to end mid-June, which was earlier than usual. Luckily, we'd had a pretty mild winter, so we didn't suck up as many snow days as some years. A lot of times, we'd be in school till like the end of June because we'd have to make up so many snow days. But this year we'd be getting out a little earlier, which was nice.

Around the end of May, this new kid moved here who was put in a couple of my classes. His name was Trevor, and he and his dad had moved here all the way from California. He seemed like a bit of a "surfer dude," but had more of an edge to him. You know what really sucked for him? His school year back home had already ended in May. When he got here though, he was enrolled in our school so that he could get "acclimated" to how things ran here before he started the new year in September. I guess he had the option of staying out and just starting up fresh in September, but his dad wanted him to get adjusted as quickly as possible.

We hit it off pretty quickly. One of the classes we had together was right before lunch, and the teacher of that class had asked me to "show Trevor the ropes" in the cafeteria. We sat together that day in lunch, and then every day after that. He was kinda sarcastic like I was, but he had way more confidence. I kinda envied that about him, but figured I could learn from it. He wasn't a dick like Josh was, but he was definitely the kind of person that other people were drawn to. Girls wanted to date him, and guys wanted to be like him. I felt like I became more popular just by hanging out with him. Everyone wanted to get to know "the new kid."

I came to find out that we had more and more in common. You wanna know what the real kicker was? He lived only with his dad for the last thirteen years. Single-parent home just like me and mom (I don't count Ricky). His mom had died when he was three. Guess how? The Twin Towers.

I couldn't believe it when he told me that. Apparently, his mom was an executive at a prestigious company in Laguna Niguel, California. But even though her office was on the west coast, she'd have to travel to the east coast every other week for business. The other office was in the Towers, and she usually had to make the trip to be in the office every other Tuesday. Of course, it wasn't one of her "off" Tuesdays on 9/11. Trevor said more than once how pissed he was at the other people in her west coast office who had been on the opposite alternating schedule and were kept from going because it was their off week. Just unbelievable. How do you explain that shit? Why couldn't she have been one of the workers who *didn't* have to go that week? It just seemed so unfair. But I could totally relate to Trevor about it. That's definitely one of the things that brought us closer.

I was really glad he had moved here. It felt nice to have someone I could actually call a *friend*. I mean, I guess it's pretty sad that before I had him, I was mostly relying on mom and Ms. Moore—two adult women—to confide in, but that was the truth. And with mom picking up more shifts at the store, and Ms. Moore definitely not being available much anymore, it was nice having Trevor to rely on. It was cool too, cuz we seemed to understand each other. He really "got" it. It was good having him to lean on considering I really didn't have anyone else. After all, Trevor could be counted on a lot more than Ms. Moore could.

# Chapter 14

I couldn't *wait* for the school year to be over. Writing that down actually made me chuckle because it sounds so much more like a kid than a teacher. I *never* had felt that way in the past. But this year, every teacher I knew couldn't wait to get out of here. And I'm sad to report that many of those teachers were looking for other jobs to get out of education. They were mailing out applications, revising their résumés, and taking interviews. Some people had already committed to new positions that they would start at the end of June. Everyone I knew seemed unhappy—actually, *beyond* unhappy. Miserable, depressed, despairing, aggravated, resentful, overwhelmed, discouraged, jaded—those words probably more accurately described what I was seeing around me. I could go on and on about the things I witnessed toward the end of that year. With all of them combined, it's amazing *anyone* signed their contract to come back in the fall.

One story worth telling is a good example of seeing teachers turn against one another. (I told you this was something that concerned me once they implemented the Michaels Model). Sure enough, two young female teachers who had been bridesmaids in each other's weddings were no longer speaking. Why? Observation scores. When final ratings were given (an average of the three observations), one girl had been rated "basic" while the other had been rated "proficient." The "basic" teacher couldn't get past the fact that her friend had been rated "proficient." (Actually, most of us couldn't understand it, either. It was a pretty well-known fact that the "basic" teacher had been a better educator than her counterpart). Interestingly, the "proficient" teacher took a new job as an administrator in another district. That made sense. Her former friend decided to leave the profession altogether. I can't emphasize enough what a loss that was to our building. I wished the "basic" teacher hadn't let the rating define her. She was one of the most dynamic teachers in our school. The kids adored her. And yet she was another casualty of the new system.

I, myself, had gotten through my other two observations. They went about as well as the one with Larry. One of the evaluations was completed by my principal, and the other had been by my supervisor. (Observations could be done by anyone in administration, so at least it hadn't been Larry all three times). That was another thing that made this process so exhausting—you never knew what the individual person was looking for when they were evaluating you. One person might really care about your questioning technique with students, one might want to see a lot of technology use, one might want to see kids doing group work the entire time—the possibilities were endless. Different evaluators had different priorities and preferences for what they deemed "important" to see in a classroom, so it was always a guessing game of trying to please whichever evaluator was coming in to observe. You had to just "play the game" by finding out what they were big on, and then making sure you did a lot of it when they were present. Talk about "disingenuous." What was *authentic* anymore about teaching? (I had always thought of teaching as "live theatre." This seemed more like "planned theatre").

Of course one of my scheduled observations had to be canceled and then rescheduled because it fell on one of the only snow days we had that year. What a waste of time that whole process had been: preparing for the lesson, attending the pre-meeting before, completing everything else that was involved...only to fall victim to a snow day. Many would ask why I couldn't just reuse the same lesson for a later date. But lessons aren't usually stand-alone. Teachers typically can't pluck one lesson out of a unit and move it to a month later. (Someone can't very well take a lesson from Puritan times and then stick it in during the Civil War). So the entire process had to be redone from start to finish. It was an exorbitant amount of work to be done all over again when it had already been done once. Talk about redundancy. And as a result, it felt like I was never seen in my classroom anymore. And I wasn't—I was always in the main office for meetings. The whole thing was a complete nightmare.

By the time my final rating reached my desk, I was so numb about the entire process that I was honestly looking at it through completely glazed-over eyes. It was like I didn't care anymore. I was indifferent. The passion was gone. At that point, I was just hoping I hadn't gotten "unsatisfactory." I would've been happy with just "basic." (And for the record, that wasn't like me at all. I was known for being a perfectionist, but here even *I* was—just shooting for average. Just trying to get by).

Apparently, my rating fell right in the middle between "basic" and "proficient." This hadn't happened to anyone else in the building (of course), so I was the first one that the administration had to have a meeting over to discuss what to do in the situation. Because the number was a raw score with decimals, they decided to round up this first time (how gracious of them). But I was warned that this would not become regular practice. (Most evaluation models actually rounded down). So I ended up with a "proficient." I didn't tell a *soul* in my building because practically everyone I knew had gotten a "basic" as their final rating, and I didn't want to be blacklisted by my colleagues. I needed to have their support and be able to lean on them because really, all we had left was each other. The paranoia set in once again, and it probably sounded crazy, but I knew it was only a matter of time before I might be on the chopping block.

One other thing I should mention is that the ratings were provided to the teacher at an end-of-year, confidential "summative review." Like other evaluation models, the Michaels Model required that every teacher meet with an administrator before the year ended to go over "performance," get our overall "rating," and provide the administrator with mounds of specified "documentation." The paperwork was justification for everything we had done during the year. It included our SAAs, data sheets of SAA scores, a printout of all of our class grades, lesson plans for every day of the year, evidence of us having "reflected" on those lessons, student attendance records, our own attendance records, a log of hours we spent achieving our own professional growth, and—I loved this one—proof that we had gone "above and beyond" attending school functions. (That could include ticket stubs to show you had gone to a school play or basketball game, receipts of products you had purchased to contribute to the bake sale, etc. I actually had attended one of my student's father's funerals. Did that show I was dedicated enough to my school? Probably not since I'm still not sure what sort of proof I could have provided. The thought of it absolutely sickened me). Needless to say, in the weeks before the end of the year, my classroom was filled with sorted piles all over the room to meet the various categories. The room was so inundated with stacks of "documentation" that I actually took a few pictures of the insanity. It was amazing that there was any room left for desks or students. Every other surface area was covered with papers.

Preparing for summative conferences sent a lot of teachers over the edge. We were spending so much time gathering evidence to show we had done our jobs during the year that we weren't able to focus on our jobs. (That sentence just made me laugh. Did anyone else see what little sense this made? It felt as though we were saying, "See? I was a 'teacher' all year." Whatever *that* meant anymore). I know personally I had spent way too many hours putting together folders and binders of documentation—time that could've been spent on coming up with new lessons or interacting with my kids. It was those extra hours spent on pointless paperwork that made me *wish* teachers were paid overtime.

With that in mind, I decided to do something I hadn't ever done. Never before had I really *scrutinized* my paycheck. But in the last two months of the school year, I did. I looked over what I was making and though it was disheartening, I forced myself to do the math to see if the time, energy, and agony had all been worth it monetarily. Prior to all of these changes, teaching had always been a matter of the heart for me. I remembered being pleasantly surprised on "payday" sometimes actually saying aloud, "Oh, yeah! I forgot they paid me for this!"—because at the time, the job had been so *fun*—too fun to get paid for. But since our state politicians felt that educators had been earning too much and had too many health benefits and other "perks," my pay had actually gone *down*. We were being asked to contribute more to those things, so as I looked back over previous paychecks, (and even previous years), I found that I was actually making less and less each year. The demands of the job were going up, but the pay was definitely going down. I felt ashamed even for doing any of this, because really, it had never before been on my radar. But now I was feeling abused and used. It was just awful. It was then that I understood why people were leaving this profession in droves. What incentive was there to *stay*? In the past I would have said that we stayed for the kids, but it felt like teaching kids was only around 5% of the job now.

There was talk of some more new initiatives coming down the pike. In addition to the two SAAs we had given this year, it looked as though a third would be implemented for next year. Observations would increase to four (which would be spread out across the entire year). The pre- and post- meetings would continue, so with the increase of four observations, that would mean we'd be spending even *more* time in the main office. (Would we ever see our kids?). And there was information making its way to us about a national standardized test that would be administered in almost all fifty states. It was a computer test that every child in America would have to take. (I wondered about kids who moved here from other countries and couldn't speak English... What would they do? And how would students with Down syndrome and other impairments take this computer test? Our school certainly didn't have enough computers to provide one to every student at a single time. How would this even work?).

As with most things in education, there was little to no information—and certainly very little comfort given to teachers.

The uncertainty alone was anxiety-provoking. We were told there would be "training" on the new test just as there had been for the new Michaels Model (which really just meant more meetings). Some of this was becoming downright comical. What was our focus anymore? What had happened to plain old solid teaching and learning? What was all of this nonsense? Was someone doing an experiment on us? With SAAs, observations, meetings, trainings, and the pending new test, it didn't seem like there was much left in a school year. Maybe robots would be implemented. Then we humans wouldn't need to get paychecks at all.

I barely recognized myself with all of this resentment and bitterness. It wasn't who I was. And it wasn't who I'd been. I had never wished for a school year to end as quickly as this one. But out of all these new changes, the one I hated *most* was the one I was starting to see in myself.

# CHAPTER 15

I ended up hanging out with Trevor *all* summer. It was a blast. We really understood each other, and it was so nice having a friend. Let me back up a sec. Before the school year had ended, I had asked Ms. Moore if I could do my usual "e-mail journal" over the summer like I had the previous year. Although she had agreed to it, I couldn't help but feel like there was some hesitation in her voice. And I just couldn't shake the feeling that every time I reached out for her, I was inconveniencing her. When summer first started, I e-mailed her once a week. The messages were really just "check-ins," telling her what I was up to, and what was going on. I had told her about Kelsey moving away, and Trevor moving in. I also asked her a lot about how *she* was doing. I didn't used to do that, but I felt obligated to. Toward the end of the year, she had seemed so down in the dumps that I felt like I should see how *she* was holding up. At first, she responded within a couple days of each submission, but then the responses got spaced out more and more. Not to mention that the feedback had gotten kinda thin. Usually I would have gotten full-page responses from her, but now it seemed I'd be lucky with a few sentences as a reply. Oh, well. Like I said, I felt like I had kinda given up on Ms. Moore. I started to lean on Trevor instead.

Trevor's dad worked a lot, so he was rarely home. The cool thing about their house was that they had a finished basement, so we pretty much spent our whole summer underground there. It really was a great "guys' hangout" area. Not only did they have a huge TV, but there was a great surround sound setup (perfect for movies or playing video games), and a bunch of leather couches to spread out on. We had movie marathons, video game wars, and buffets of fast food. It was so much fun.

My mom didn't even seem to mind that I was hanging out there so much. I think she was almost relieved that I was "off her hands" for a bit having found a new buddy. Of course, Ricky made it known that he thought the two of us were "wasting away our lives" and he usually made snide comments when I'd leave the house to go over to Trevor's. One time Trevor skateboarded over to our house cuz we were gonna go to the local convenience store before heading over to his house, and Ricky couldn't resist giving us both a hard time when we left.

Once we were clear down the road, Trevor stated the obvious. "Dude, why's your stepdad such a dick?"

I was riding my bike alongside him skateboarding, and I felt my shoulders tighten while hunched over my handlebars. "Um, I don't know. He's just always been an asshole, I guess."

"C'mon—there's gotta be more to it than that. Has he always been that way?"

I didn't really wanna go there, so I tried to change the subject. "Yeah, whatever. It's no big deal. Let's get the chips and get back to your house. We gotta get to the next level of *Demon Hunter.*"

"All right. You're so tense, man. I got something that'll calm your ass down."

It was that day that Trevor introduced me to the wonderful world of pot.

---

At first, I felt like a complete idiot because I honestly didn't know shit about smoking. I had always heard people talking about "inhaling" and that there were people who looked like jackasses for not knowing how to. Trevor was a good teacher. He had been smoking since he was twelve, so he was already a pro. But he didn't make me feel like an idiot for not knowing what I was doing. When I first started, I didn't really feel anything. The more we started doing it, though, the better it made me feel.

That became the usual routine. I'd go over to Trevor's, we'd smoke, play video games or watch TV, and then we'd eat a bunch of bad shit. I'm not sure where he got his stash. Some of it I think he'd somehow gotten here from California. But I think once he was here, he'd started to establish some "connections" (if that's what you even call it). I don't really know what made me first start it. I mean, I'd been to some parties and stuff where it had been offered, but for whatever reason, I hadn't ever tried. When Trevor said it would probably help me chill out a bit about stuff, though, I figured why not? I mean, it was like a plant, right?

That's one thing I really liked about it—it helped me to open up a lot more. Weird as it sounds, I found that I'd talk more about shit that mattered to me—not the superficial stuff. Trevor and I would get into these deep conversations about life. We'd talk about everything. It was like nothing was off-limits. We talked about 9/11, our dead parents, our live parents, school, girls, everything. It was crazy that I'd only known him a couple months, but could tell him pretty much everything I could've told Ms. Moore. Soon, I was sharing stuff I hadn't *even* shared with Ms. Moore. I felt a little guilty about that because she had always been my confidante, but frankly, she was nowhere to be found.

The other thing, too, was that it wasn't threatening. I don't know—there was something about the pot that would almost make us forget shit after. It was like I could tell Trevor a whole bunch of stuff that was bothering me, but then the next time I'd see him, he'd basically forgotten it anyway, so it was never held against me or anything. It's not like he'd bring it up again, or use it against me, or make me feel stupid. I could just tell him stuff freely, and then follow up with more stuff the next time without any negative judgment or anything.

I eventually told him the stuff about Ricky. There were a lot of reasons why I hated that scumbag, but there was also one really big reason. Kind of a deep, dark secret. No one knew about this—especially not my mom—but when I was little, Ricky stayed home with me while my mom worked. He had lost his job, so between the ages of like 6-10 (as far as I can remember), he was like the "stay-at-home" parent (or what I'd call a total "deadbeat" in his case), and my mom worked full-time. I think she thought I was in good hands, but that's so far from the truth.

What she didn't know was that he'd often bring women into the house. When I was really young, I didn't quite understand why they were there. He would tell me they were his "special friends" and that "Mommy could never know." As I got older and started to understand what sex and stuff was, I would get really pissed and he and I would get into shouting matches. He would threaten me a lot that if I ever told my mom, she would be devastated, fall apart, and not be able to go on with her life (since she had already suffered a broken heart from the death of my real dad). He'd say that she was so weak she'd probably commit suicide, and then I would be left without a mom, and that *he* would be my sole guardian raising me. As a little kid, that was great motivation. I was scared shitless of losing my mom after already losing my real dad, and I was scared even more of being stuck with just Ricky for the rest of my life.

Not only did he guilt me into believing that my mom would be gone from my life forever, but he would also "physically ensure" that I'd keep my mouth shut. You name it—belts, electrical cords, furniture—any or all would be used to hurt me. He'd make sure to hit me in areas that would be covered by clothing—and warned me that again, mom would be gone if she ever saw any marks on me. That was even worse—he had said that if I ever showed anyone the evidence (including adults at school), he'd tell authorities that it had been my *mom* who had done it—and that again, he'd make sure I'd be taken away from her.

This stopped after I turned eleven. I was old enough to fight back, and when we had gotten into another one of our shouting matches, my mom happened to walk in right as I took my first-ever punch at Ricky. Though she was horrified, Ricky assured her that everything was ok, and that we had just gotten into a "little argument" and that it was "all his fault." Man, could that guy turn on the charm. I had never seen him so sweet before. He even went to the grocery store and brought home flowers for her. But it pretty much stopped after that. I think he knew he was dangerously close to getting caught (both with the women and the abuse), and at that point I think he knew that I was old enough and smart enough to start fighting back. Shortly after the incident, he got a new job and was in the house a lot less, thank God. As you can imagine, I avoided him at all costs—which may have contributed to my obsession with *Demon Hunter* and other violent video games—it was a good way to get the anger out.

I didn't really harp on any of this as I got into my teen years. I knew enough fucked-up kids at school to know that most kids had shit going on in their families. I figured what I had faced was pretty normal. Sometimes the feelings would come up in my head, but I mostly just pushed them as far down as I could and tried to forget about them. There was nothing to be done about any of it anyway. It was all in the past. It wasn't affecting me now.

Anyway, I told Trevor some of the Ricky stuff. It did feel good getting a lot of it off my chest. I appreciated being able to confide in him—especially cuz he didn't make me feel like I was crazy, or worse—act all *sorry* for me. I hate when people give you that look like, "Aww, you poor, pitiful, pathetic thing." I didn't need anyone's sympathy. But it felt good to finally tell someone those buried secrets. I had never told anyone before.

Trevor did say he was sorry that I had gone through all that for so many years (to which I kinda just brushed off with my usual, "whatever, whatever"). But he followed up with *his* usual, "Listen, if you decide you wanna blast the motherfucker someday, lemme know.

I *know* people," to which I laughed pretty hard. (Although I didn't doubt that he was being serious. Trevor had this way about him that made me think he probably *did* know some people in what I'd call the "underworld." I mean, he hadn't lived here that long before he knew enough people to score pot. In some ways, I was a little scared of him).

Around the end of July, I went over his house to find him sound asleep on one of the leather couches in the basement. It took a while to wake him up, but eventually he sat up and then his face perked up excitedly.

"Dude, if you think the pot makes ya feel good, you should try the shit I tried last night. Holy shit." He went on to tell me about his latest discovery: cocaine. That shit made me *real* nervous. I mean, I'm no prude, but that shit seemed a bit overboard. I told him I appreciated the offer, but that if it was ok with him, I'd just stick to the herbal shit. He shrugged, but didn't push. We resumed our usual TV marathons and junk food (talk about someone having "the munchies" after the kind of night *he* had). I felt a little uneasy about the whole thing, but I tried to just forget about it. I obviously couldn't tell my mom about this—there was no way in hell she'd ever let me back over here. Too bad Ms. Moore *was* "no more." I bet *she* would've known what to do.

# CHAPTER 16

I spent the summer in mourning. That sounds overly dramatic, but it was the truth. Most teachers I knew had to work a summer job in order to make ends meet. I was one of the lucky ones who didn't have to because my husband made enough money that I could take the summers "off." Interestingly, though, there were so many meetings and trainings we had to attend during the summer that I wondered how anyone was able to "work" elsewhere. We didn't get paid for attending these required sessions, either. But the district "graciously" told us that the hours would count toward our "professional growth"—and that would be found quite favorable on the Michaels Model. Goody.

And there *was* plenty of work that summer to keep teachers preparing for the upcoming year. When I spoke to my colleagues, most of them were spending time recreating their SAAs or adding their third newly required one, redesigning old units and lessons, revamping their overall teaching styles, taking classes on how to increase their observation scores, preparing for the new national test that we heard would be implemented, and dreading what new demands would continue to be placed on us. Some of them continued their search for other careers: redoing their résumés, sending them out, asking around, and just looking to get out of education altogether.

When I say I was "mourning," what I really meant was that I was questioning everything around me, and was *really* missing my students. I felt like I wasn't the same teacher anymore. I used to have time to talk to kids, to counsel them, to journal with them, to connect with them, to feel like I had made a difference in their lives. At the end of the school year, one of my former students had come to visit me, having been home from college. She was about to start her senior year; I couldn't believe she had already been out of high school for over three years. One of the things she remarked was that I didn't seem like myself. My classroom didn't look the same to her, she said I seemed different, and she was surprised that I wasn't surrounded by kids. Her younger brother would be starting high school the coming fall, and she was hoping he would have me as a teacher. Little did she know I was *dreading* the coming school year. Or actually, maybe she *did* know. I think she could tell how unhappy I was—that I was questioning my career and whether I should even continue it. It hurt me deeply that I seemed so different to her. Here she was, having been out of the building for the last three years, and after spending fifteen minutes with me, she knew that I was a different person—and quite a different teacher.

During the summer I decided that I would give up the journal-writing thing. I just wouldn't have the time for it with all the new demands. There was no way I'd be able to keep up with responding to the kids knowing what was coming down the pike. And my attitude was, if I couldn't do them *right*—the way they *should* be done—then I didn't want to do them at all. I decided that I would still collect from any former students who wanted to continue journaling. I felt they should be "grandfathered" in. But any new incoming freshman, I wouldn't even start the process. I hoped that by only offering it to former students, it would cut down on my workload considerably (since there were only some who continued writing to me after their freshman year ended). But I couldn't shake how guilty it made me feel. It seemed so unfair to any future students that only former students would be permitted to submit. I'd never get to foster those deep relationships with the new kids—and they would be denied the opportunity to write to someone who cared about them, and who was rooting for them. In a way, I figured they wouldn't know that they were missing anything since they had never been a part of it. And besides, with all the new testing and demands, the kids would probably be so swamped, they wouldn't have the time to write for fun, anyway. But it still broke my heart. Would those kids ever learn the power of free-writing, or what a great outlet it served to vent and get things out? They would probably only ever write for the formal sake of writing: probably for tests and…more tests.

Speaking of journals, I was probably mourning the loss of Petey most of all. I had agreed to "e-mail journal" with him over the summer, but I could tell he was distancing himself from me. And I couldn't blame him. I knew I couldn't keep up with writing back, or offering as much feedback as I had previously. It was the worst feeling knowing he couldn't count on me. We had made so much progress in terms of him starting to dig deeper and divulge more of his life in his journals. His sophomore year, he had shared so much more with me than he had his freshman year. He had started to dig beneath the surface: telling me about the dynamics in his family, the loss of his father, dealing with his stepfather, feeling lost without true friends, how he had gotten suspended, life lessons he had learned in my class and was applying to his life… It had been *amazing* watching Petey's growth. He had matured a great deal, and I think the reflection he had done in his writing had helped him so much in everyday life. And yet I barely had the time to respond to him anymore. I felt so guilty. I felt mad at the system. Was this what they were trying to create? Teachers who could no longer be there for their students? That sure was how it felt.

There were other "Peteys" I felt I was letting down, but him most of all. The batch of kids I still had writing to me were the types who I felt had strong enough support systems in place that if I wasn't available, they would have others to lean on. But not Petey. Although his mom seemed like a good woman, I felt that she was the only person he really had in life. Having me was a good back-up. And at this point, I couldn't guarantee that I would be there anymore. It felt like I had lied to all of my kids when I told them I wasn't just their freshman teacher, but their "forever teacher." I had barely been able to keep up with the journals of freshman students I had during the school year. I just didn't have the *time*. I was "too busy" keeping up with the new demands being thrown at us. And I was sick of being "busy." I didn't want to give up Petey or my other kids. It wasn't right. What if they needed a trusted adult? What if they needed me and I couldn't be there because I was in a post-observation meeting, or compiling data spreadsheets for SAAs, or getting observed, or proctoring new tests, or attending this training or that meeting? Was there to be any interaction with students anymore? Not the kind I wanted or found valuable. Was I just a teacher occasionally at the front of the room giving tests and barking new orders? Maybe I wasn't fit for the job anymore. I felt like I was becoming more of a disservice to the kids than a guiding light.

Throughout the summer I had several nightmares worrying about kids who might fall through the cracks since they wouldn't have teachers who had time to care about them. Many of those dreams had Petey in them. My dentist even verified that I was grinding my teeth at night—stress dreams, he said. My anxiety was clearly being manifested and coming out while I slept. It might have sounded weird, but teaching had always been so *personal* to me. Maybe I *did* take this stuff personally, but I thought that was the whole point. Petey was one of those kids I had always worried about falling through the cracks. And I was starting to feel it tangibly happening. The most hopeless part was feeling completely helpless—knowing there wasn't a thing I could do about it.

# CHAPTER 17

I know it probably sounds kinda pathetic, but at the time that my junior year started, I felt really alone. I felt like I had no one to confide in about stuff. Toward the end of summer, Trevor had gotten more involved in some of the heavier shit. He was still around, but he wasn't all there. The coke seemed to make him hyper and bouncing around at times, and then he would crash. He stopped being fun to be around. We had hung out like every day that summer, but the last week or two of it, I was only over there maybe two or three times. He was either on his phone or going over to one of his suppliers' (that's what I called them anyway). I was surprised that his dad didn't seem to notice. He was either working or spending time with his new girlfriend. Trevor didn't seem to like her much. He certainly didn't share the hatred I had for Ricky, but I guess any kid wouldn't want their real parent ever being replaced by someone else.

I met one of the guys Trevor was spending a lot of time with and getting the weed and coke from. His name was Manny. He was 24 and it was obvious that Trevor idolized him. I started to stay away a bit more because truthfully, Manny made me kind of nervous. It's not like I was a nerd or anything—I mean, I knew of kids who were older than I was who had done harder drugs and stuff. But Manny and all of his crew seemed really shady. The one or two times I had met them, my stomach was in knots the whole time. They were a little pushy about stuff, and Trevor seemed to go right along with it. It was weird—I had always thought that *Trevor* was the one who was ballsy and fearless and strong—but in front of these guys, he was like a little mouse. I tried to keep my distance, and even though I had never really looked forward to a school year starting, I was kinda happy it was just about to so that things would get busy and I wouldn't feel pressured to be around those guys.

I was also hoping that once the year started, Trevor would cut out some of the shit and just go through the motions with school. But I was wrong. He was absent a *lot* during the first few weeks. I was actually kinda worried. The drug shit was totally taking over his life. It sucked too, cuz I had really thought of him as a friend. I'm not sure what kept me from getting involved with all the hard shit. I guess it was just that I kept seeing the disappointed look on my mom's face if she knew I was doing that kind of stuff. I also knew that even though I hadn't been in touch with her that much this summer, Ms. Moore would've been disappointed in me, too.

I stopped in to see her after the first week of school was over. I figured she'd be swamped in the beginning as usual, so I hoped she'd be more available once things settled down a bit. The thing is, though, I *didn't* see Ms. Moore—at all. Every time I went by her classroom, the lights were out, the door was locked, and she was nowhere in sight. And the creepy part was, her classroom looked like a ghost town. It used to be so colorful and chaotic, you would've thought a traveling circus had been through it each day. This year, I don't think I saw one poster hanging up. The room was totally gray. It almost looked as though she hadn't been there yet to decorate it.

There wasn't even any *student* work hanging up—and there *always* had been. She loved displaying kids' stuff. I almost thought she had taken early retirement and another person had been assigned to her room. But I saw the nameplate on her desk, and it still said her name, so I assumed she was still employed in our building.

I was pretty disappointed she was nowhere to be found because honestly, I wanted to talk to her about Trevor—about what was going on. Even though she didn't know him because she hadn't had him as a student, I felt uneasy about the whole thing, and I knew I'd feel better if I could just talk to her about it. I think I was mourning the loss of his friendship. It almost felt like I was going through a break-up with a girl. I didn't know if I should mention the drug thing to Ms. Moore—I was gonna be pretty vague about that part because I figured she might have to report that kind of thing if she had knowledge about it. But I just wanted someone I could go to. I was kinda pissed that she was never around anymore. She had always told us we could go to her with anything.

The third week of school, I decided I might stop by during the flex lunch period. (I mean, the woman had to eat, right?). Since the whole school stopped for lunch, I was hoping she might be around. When I got to her classroom, she was actually in there for once. Shocker. But of course, it looked like she was gathering up her things getting ready to leave yet again.

"Ms. Moore!" I exclaimed. "Oh, my gosh, it's so great to see you! How are you? Do you have time to talk?" I waited expectantly, hoping she would drop everything and be able to talk—like she used to.

"Oh...*hey* Petey," she said almost sympathetically. "Gee, ya know, I don't really have time right now. They're asking English and math teachers to report to the auditorium for a meeting. But I hope you had a great summer. Maybe we can catch up some other time?"

"Oh," I said, feeling a mixture of sadness and resentment. "Um, ok. I just really could use your advice on something. Maybe I could write to you and then you could get back to me on your own time?"

"Uhhh...yeah, that would probably be ok," she said totally unconvincingly. I started to look around the room for the journal drop-off box. It was nowhere to be found.

"Um, where's the drop-off box? I don't see it anywhere."

"Oh, I'm not doing them anymore." She sighed. "I just can't keep up with the responses. I don't have the time anymore." I felt like I had been punched in the stomach. She didn't exactly say that she didn't have time for *us* anymore, but that's exactly how I took it.

"Oh, uh, okaaay. I won't bother you then." At that, she seemed to soften a bit.

"I mean, I plan to keep doing them for kids I already had. I just can't take on any new students. I'm just..." Her voice trailed off. "I just can't do it all."

"I understand," I said, even though I didn't. "Well then, I'll try to write it all down I guess, and then should I just drop it off to you personally?" In my head, I could hear myself saying, *Yeah, right. As if I'll ever catch a sighting of you in this school again.*

"Uh, sure, that would be fine," she said quickly, with a wave of her hand. "I'm sorry, Petey, but I really gotta get down to the auditorium."

"Sure," I said. And with that, she power-walked to the door, flicked off the lights, and left me standing there alone. I felt so completely blown off, I stood there with my mouth hanging open. Who the hell was this woman? She was *not* the teacher so many of us had known and loved. It was like she couldn't be bothered. I felt awful. I felt alone. I felt kicked aside. I mean, teachers were supposed to be people we could *go* to, could *count* on. It was like she had torn up her teacher card. I honestly didn't know if I should even bother writing to her. What would be the point?

And no more journals? What the hell was *that*? She had given up accepting new students' submissions? Journal writing was like the whole basis of her class! It made us *think*—it made us reflect. It made us learn more about ourselves and all the shit going on around us. Had she forgotten that? I was so disappointed. I felt abandoned. I felt like I had no one. Who would help me get through the school year? My mom obviously couldn't come with me to school every day—and even so, that would be kind of pitiful. I didn't know who Ms. Moore had become—but I certainly didn't recognize her anymore.

# CHAPTER 18

That third week of school on my way to the auditorium, I felt like I was going to vomit. I was running late to the staff meeting, and I had just been so completely curt with Petey. I couldn't stand the look in his eyes. He looked so hurt, so confused, so alone. But I just *didn't* have the time to speak to him then. I felt like I was running ragged—being pulled in twelve different directions. How could I please everyone? There were so many demands and just not enough time. I felt like I was going insane. Maybe I needed medication.

The meeting, specifically for English and math teachers, was to provide information on the new national test we had heard would be implemented during the year. As expected, this meant that in the coming weeks and months, there would be workshops to attend on it (for training of course) which most of us just interpreted as less time being in our classrooms with our kids. We would attend conferences to learn the ins and outs of the test—what the layout was and how it worked, but virtually no information on how we could help our kids prepare for it.

Apparently, this test was being looked at as incredibly innovative because it would be entirely computer-based. Kids would answer multiple-choice questions and essay prompts all on the computer—clicking and typing away. For the math portion, even the *calculator* would be on the computer screen. They would have to solve equations, utilize formulas, and complete open-ended responses all on the computer. It was nuts. For this year, only English and math would be tested in all grades (except kindergarten and grade twelve), but in future years, the other subjects would be added. And of course, it would become a graduation requirement. For a moment, I imagined a second-grader collapsing in tears, not knowing how to use the calculator on the computer screen. (Talk about test anxiety).

The new testing initiative was called the National Assessment for Student Achievement, or, for short, the "NASA" (yup—like the space program. Maybe they thought it was a subliminal message to the public: our kids are at such a high level of intelligence, taking this test will put them on par with rocket scientists). Meanwhile, we were still required to create and administer the three Student Achievement Assessments (SAAs) during the year. Those weren't being replaced by the NASA testing. "Student achievement" and "assessment" must have been new buzz words the powers-that-be loved and wanted to see more of in education. But how many tests could kids take? Weren't they being tested *enough*?

Since NASAs were entirely computer-based, I couldn't help but feel that once again, this was a money-making scheme. It was as though schools were being used for "big business." To me, it seemed everyone was looking to cash in and make a buck. I imagined all the major software companies making bids to create and administer the tests. Different politicians would be vying for the best programs to help boost their campaigns. Major educational testing firms would want to get in on the action as it would mean big bucks for them.

Somehow, the whole initiative just felt crooked and corrupt. It wasn't at all put in place for the benefit of the kids. What was the *real* point behind this whole thing? What was the driving force? Feelings of disgust started to creep up and overwhelm me.

To make things worse, after this first initial year (the "pilot year"), these tests would be tied into teachers' salaries, ratings, and retention. And all of this information would be released to the public. So if you had a class that happened to perform poorly on the test, your job would be on the line. You'd probably take a major pay cut. And you certainly wouldn't be getting "Advanced" ratings on your Michaels Model Evaluation. I thought of other professions for a moment. Did anyone cut a doctor's pay if the patient didn't follow his instructions? Did a grocery store cashier get fired if a coupon couldn't be used at checkout? None of it seemed rational.

Yet again, I felt sick and defeated. How could we possibly take on one more thing? Our plates were already full. Was I supposed to spend my whole school year trying to teach what little information I knew about the test for the sole purpose of keeping my job, keeping my ratings up, and making sure my pay was secure? How selfish was that! Were my students just a means to an end? My purpose and direction was utterly obliterated. I felt so lost. What was even my *purpose* and role as the teacher anymore?

The meeting concluded with informing us that since math and English were the tested subjects, we would naturally be the ones administering the exam on test days. (I couldn't help but note that we felt like *literal* "test subjects" in a horrible lab experiment). Schools would be given thirty full days to administer all components (the range of days would supposedly provide ample time for students to be rotated and processed through the number of computers in the building). I wondered how schools in lower socioeconomic areas would be able to accomplish this—especially those lacking in technology. We had a decent number of computers in our building, but even we would probably be short. (Our own district had spent money last year buying some new computers with the money teachers had started contributing to health care. I had heard of some districts who had used that money on new computers for staff use; however, today we were told that staff members in those districts would be asked to surrender those computers for testing since there wouldn't be enough of them). Since most of our school's computers were located in the library, this meant the library would have to be "closed" for testing for at least an entire month. So much for students being able to go there at any time. Would they ever learn research skills? Ever check out books? Ever type essays? Maybe libraries weren't considered important anymore.

Administering the test meant that those teachers wouldn't be in their classrooms during it. There would be substitute teachers carrying on "instruction" while we were busy testing. (The plan was to have students test alphabetically by last name, so there might still be remaining students in our classrooms during the period while others were in the library testing). The disruption to the school calendar and master schedule was just absurd. We were also told that those considered "highly responsible" teachers would be contacted individually, as they would be needed not only to administer exams, but also to attend several meetings to create the testing schedule, compile class rosters, and establish computer rotations. It felt as though we were being punished. Immediately "Lazy Larry" came to my mind. I knew the building administrators would never make him part of this initiative because only the people who did the "real" work could be trusted to handle such a responsibility. Therefore, teachers like us would be pulled from our classrooms all the time because we were reliable. (Talk about how "no good deed goes unpunished." The message was, if you were dependable and good at your job, you were punished by being assigned to this nonsense). You should've seen the body language of all the teachers present in the auditorium. They were hunched over their laps with looks of anguish on their faces. Some of them had dark circles under their eyes already, and we were only in the third week of the school year.

When we were dismissed, there actually was no rumbling among the staff. Just silence. And sadness, akin to people departing a funeral. My shoulders were heavy as I trudged back to my own classroom. I kept thinking about Petey and the other kids. What effect would this have on them? *More* testing? I actually felt momentarily relieved that I had decided against accepting journals this year. Now it was confirmed that there was *no* way I could've kept up with them. I wouldn't even be around anymore to read them. And why would it matter anyway? I probably wouldn't be in my classroom teaching much this year. I'm sure a substitute would get more face-time with my students than I would.

Once again, the familiar idea returned to my mind that maybe I should leave teaching altogether. This wasn't what I signed up for. This wasn't what *any* of us signed up for. If everyone felt the way I did, schools would be emptied of teachers. I felt like I was betraying Petey—like I was betraying *all* of my students by signing up for a job where I thought I could be there for them, only to find out I could never keep that promise. Disappointment consumed me.

When I got back to my classroom, I caught sight of a poster I had gotten from The Globe Theatre many years ago. It was lying in a stack of other posters I hadn't even had the time to decorate my walls with yet. It was brightly colored and had several phrases on it that Shakespeare was known for coining. My eyes met with one that took on a new meaning in that moment: "what's done is done." And it truly *was*. That's how everything felt. There was no fighting these new changes. They were all going in to effect and there was not a thing we could do to stop them. What was done was truly *done. I* felt done, too.

# CHAPTER 19

I thought about writing down how I was feeling about everything and submitting a new journal to Ms. Moore, but every time I was about to start writing, I kept asking myself what the point was. It seemed as though Ms. Moore had abandoned me—and all of her students for that matter. She certainly wasn't the teacher we knew anymore. And I didn't want to feel like an annoyance or burden to her. The last thing I wanted was to get scraps of someone's attention—what would be the point?

I guess I appeared pretty mopey at home. Even *Demon Hunter* wasn't cutting it anymore. I just felt lost—like I had no one. It was weird. In my new English class this year, my teacher had mentioned that one of the recurring themes we would see in the literature we read in this curriculum would be the power of what she called "human connection"—this idea that people needed other people. It was a necessity of life. She said that the characters we'd be studying would all yearn for and need other people to connect with. And the fact was that we *all* needed to feel connected to *someone* in order to feel like we had purpose, meaning, and a reason to be on this planet. The awful part was, I *didn't* feel connected to anyone. I felt like I was floundering. I was pretty much alone. I mean, who did I *really* have in my life that I could go to? Honestly.

It all came to a head on a Saturday in mid-October. Ricky started in on me, complaining that I was acting all mopey and depressed.

"What the fuck is *wrong* with you? Come *on*—you're a teenager for Christ's sake. Your life is not that hard. Fucking suck it up."

"Why don't you shut the fuck up, Ricky? You're a do-nothing who mooches off my mom. You have no idea what's going on in my life, so fucking stay out of it."

"Hey! You don't talk to me that way in my house."

"It's not *your* house. It's my mother's—ya know, the one you cheated on for *years* when she first let you stay here? You're despicable."

When I whipped around to head for my room, I came face-to-face with my mother. I hadn't realized she had walked in. I thought she was in the shower. The look on her face was a combination of shock, anger, and utter betrayal. I felt my stomach drop to the floor.

"Peter," she said, her mouth still gaping open, "what are you talking about?"

I stood there for a moment, silent. It felt like the floor was sliding out from underneath me. I knew she hadn't known about any of that, and this wasn't how I ever planned on her finding out. But the truth was, she had to know. So I turned and pointed my finger at Ricardo.

"Why don't *you* tell her, Ricky?" I asked, moving to stand by my mom, facing him.

"He's making shit up, Maria. He's a teenaged boy. You know he always does this to cause problems between us. He doesn't know what he's talking about."

My mom seemed to think for a moment, then turned to me.

"Why would you say something like this, Peter? It's very hurtful, and quite an accusation to make." She put her hands on her hips and tilted her head at me, eyebrows raised.

My mouth fell open in bewilderment. "Are you taking *his side?*" I screamed at the highest octave my voice would go.

"Well, what proof do you—" she started to say before I put my hand up to interrupt her.

"Ya know what? I'm outta here. If you're gonna choose that asshole over your *own son,* then I have nothing else to say," I said choking out the last four words. I could feel my voice starting to crack, and my eyes had begun to fill with tears. Ugh, I wish there hadn't been evidence of that. I *hate* that I looked so weak in that moment. I ran off to my room, and started throwing things into an overnight bag. I wasn't sure where I was going yet, but I knew I had to get out of there.

A few tears streamed down my face. I quickly wiped them away with the back of my hand. I didn't have time to be upset. Flashes of my real dad—what memories I had left of him—zipped through my head. I felt sick. I wished I could join him wherever he was—heaven, hell. Anything was better than this hell on earth.

I could hear my mother calling after me, but I wasn't responding. Then she and Ricky started to argue. I threw some clothes and underwear into my duffel bag, and quickly grabbed my toothbrush from the bathroom. Then I slid out my window onto the grass, picked up my bike that had been leaning on the side of the house, and started to ride toward Trevor's. He hadn't been the greatest friend lately, but it felt like he was all I had left. I didn't know where else to go.

My head was swarming with thoughts as I rode there. *How could she not believe me? Why didn't she try to stop me? If that's how she feels, fuck both of them. I'm done.* When I got to Trevor's house, his dad was actually home—with the new girlfriend, of course.

"Hey, Mr. Nolan," I said as politely as I could, even though my head felt like it was raging. "I, um…I'm a little embarrassed, but I had kind of a blowout with my parents. Would it be ok with you if I stayed here for a day or two till things cool off?" I knew I was actually lying because as far as I was concerned, I'd be staying here way longer than that.

"Sure, kid," he said, barely looking up from his girlfriend. He was staring at her with googly eyes, twirling a strand of her hair. "Do they know you're here?" he asked, absently.

"Oh, yeah," I lied, although I figured my mom would guess that I came here.

"Make yourself at home. I think Trevor's actually still sleeping. His friends dropped him off pretty late last night."

*Great*, I thought, picturing Manny and crew dumping Trevor off in the driveway. But I nodded, and headed to the end of the hall where Trevor's room was. I knocked lightly, and then slowly turned the doorknob. I was a bit surprised he was still sleeping. It was already afternoon.

"Hey, dude, you sleeping?" I asked, pushing on the lump that was buried under the comforter. "Trevor." I rolled my eyes and started to pull back the blankets. Must've been some late night. He was on his stomach, head under the pillow, still wearing the clothes he'd gone out in last night. I tugged on his shoulder a bit, the fabric of his shirt pulling enough that my hand made contact with his flesh. It was freezing and his skin felt drenched. "Yo, man," I said louder, starting to panic. I pulled the pillow off the bed and rolled him over. He was soaked and his eyes were closed. There were remnants of foam at the corners of his mouth. *Oh, my God. Oh, my God. Is he dead? Holy shit.*

"Mr. Nolan!" I shrieked, not even recognizing my own voice. "Oh, my God—help! Something's wrong with Trevor!"

———————————————

I think I told you earlier that junior year was the beginning of the end. But I guess the end had started long before this.

# CHAPTER 20

On a Friday night in October, I put myself to bed pretty early, around 7:00. I felt so exhausted from everything going on at school, my body and mind just crashed. But even though I was usually one to turn in early, it was more of a curse than a blessing because that's when the thoughts would start. I would lie awake for *hours* just replaying in my head what was going on in my school and education in general. The thoughts would just swirl around, consuming every moment I stayed awake. I'm ashamed to admit that sometimes I would even respond to the thoughts aloud. Sometimes I'd be preparing a defense in case Lazy Larry gave me a bad review, or I would talk aloud to the SAAs, telling them that they weren't measuring *anything*. I felt like a nut. Maybe I was turning in to one.

The list of thoughts—or, *ruminations* I should probably call them—covered a wide range of topics. I thought about the Michaels Model and some of the absurdities listed on it. Since there would be four required observations starting this year, I was probably due for an evaluation any day now. In one of the categories, in order to get "Advanced," the scoresheet explained that if the lesson was good enough, the students themselves would "initiate their own insightful inquiries relevant to the material being presented." I actually laughed in bed right then. These were *teenagers* we were talking about. Most of us were just thrilled if they showed up and stayed *awake* during the school day. And what made an inquiry "insightful"? That seemed pretty subjective. How was *that* quantifiable? Maybe we could pay our kids ahead of time and stage the whole thing. Who said bribes weren't allowed if it meant getting a top score?

That was another thing—a *score*. Over and over in my head, I kept repeating to myself that teachers were getting a "score" on how they presented a lesson. A score. The actual thought of it seemed so ridiculous, anyone outside of education probably would've thought we were joking if we told them about that. It was amazing that so many of these initiatives were being put in place to supposedly "improve teaching" and "make teachers better." Yet nothing about it was encouraging. There was no positive affirmation. No acknowledgement of a job well done—only things we did wrong, how awful we all were, and how we had to dramatically change things to improve since we were so terrible. It was as though we were always being set up to "play defense." There was no collaboration or teamwork anymore—just an evaluator whose sole function on the planet was to be the arbiter of our worth. At this rate, there would be no teachers left. We'd either end up leaving before they could fire us, or they simply *would* fire us. Who would be left to teach our kids?

"Honey?" I heard my husband call, which abruptly interrupted my thoughts. I could hear the front door close behind him. Climbing out from under the comforter, I sat up in bed just as Will peered in, opening the bedroom door slowly. I was grateful for the interruption.

"Hey," he said looking concerned. "You turning in early? It's 7:00."

"Hi," I said, pulling the covers around me so snugly only my head was exposed. I felt like a little kid needing a teddy bear or something. "Yeah, I'm just..." my voice trailed off. "I'm just," I started again. My eyes started to fill with tears.

"Hon, you need to stop this. It's just a job. You can *quit*. I can support both of us. I hate seeing you this upset. I don't wanna bury my wife before she's 110 because her job drove her to an early grave."

I smiled. "I don't think I'll live till 110 at this rate anyway," I chuckled. Will always knew what to say. He had been telling me for probably the last year and a half that if I wanted to quit teaching, everything would be ok—that he made enough money to support us both. That he just wanted to see me happy. He said all the right things. And yet, I still felt so depressed.

"I mean it," he said sternly. "Enough already. Who do I need to kill? Is it Lazy Larry this time?" His usually calm blue eyes flashed with pretended rage for a moment. I loved those blue eyes. They always mimicked what was going on around us: they'd be stormy if things were stormy, and tranquil if things were serene. But they always had these little flicks of yellow that glinted hope. Those were *always* there.

I smiled again. "Everything's just so different now. I mean, I'm never around anymore. We're all having to help out with the testing schedule for NASAs, not to mention we all have our three SAAs to do, and observations have already started. When do we get to *teach* anymore? I feel like I barely even know my kids this year. I don't even know all their names yet, and it's October. That never happens. You know me—I pride myself on knowing their names by the second day of school. But they keep pulling us for meetings and stuff, and I'm just never around. I've got another pointless conference on Monday, too."

"You oughta get 'Teacher of the Year' just for knowing what all those abbreviations stand for!" he exclaimed. I laughed. I had gotten "Teacher of the Year" twice during my tenure, but I was pretty sure I'd never be honored with that again.

He continued. "But seriously. I mean, you always used to say that the most important thing was to 'reach' the kids before you could teach them anything. And now it's like the job doesn't even allow you to do that. And that's the part you *love*. So why don't you just get out of this racket? I can see how much you're struggling. I've never seen you hate your work before."

"You're right about that—there *is* no reaching anymore. It's so sad. But you've got a point. Maybe I *should* just call it quits."

"Hey, while we're at it, how's Petey doing? I haven't heard you mention him in a while."

I felt the familiar pang in my stomach and my eyes filled with tears again. "Ya know what? I honestly *don't* know. I don't *know* how Petey's doing. I don't have *time* to know—or time to care. I'm too busy trying to keep up with all the demands they keep throwing at us." I paused, before admitting, "I actually gave up on the journals this year. I can't take on any new ones. I just can't give them the time they require and deserve."

He sighed. "I was wondering why the house looked so clean without piles of notebooks all over," he teased. He was quiet for a moment, then said, "Listen, it sounds like a broken system. It's totally different from when you started. Things have changed. Why don't you think it over, and if things don't get better, put in for resignation at the end of the year."

We were both silent for a moment. I nodded, not saying anything.

"In the meantime, how 'bout a pizza? I'm starving." He patted my knee, smiled, and then headed for the kitchen. I pushed the covers off and swept my legs out to extend my feet down to the carpet. As I stood up, I thought of Petey. A flash of panic came over me for a moment. I'm not sure why, but I felt scared for him at that moment. I hoped everything was ok. Then again, even if it wasn't, it's not like I would've had the time to do anything about it.

# CHAPTER 21

They said it was an overdose. It was the first time Trevor had ever tried heroin. We had been at the hospital since I found him. Of course I ended up having to call my mom to tell her where I was. (I hated that. My plan had been to never talk to either of them again. I hated being the one to give in. But at that point, pride was the least of my problems).

By Sunday evening, the news was pretty final. Trevor was brain dead. The amount in his system was too much for his body to handle. The doctors said it was typical with "first-time tries" of heroin: the "first time" was often the *last* time for many. They confirmed that there was really no hope. At that, I watched Mr. Nolan crumble. I had never seen a grown man so hysterical. He was literally on his knees, holding the hands of the lead doctor, begging him for different news. Something else. Some shred of hope. It reminded me of my mom on 9/11. She had been the same way. Mr. Nolan's girlfriend stood next to him, her hands on his shoulders. The only thing left to do was pull the plug.

Mom picked me up that night. We were silent the whole car ride, except for her asking to make sure I had never gotten involved in any of the heavier shit. I assured her I hadn't. I didn't know what to think. I guess I was in shock—utter disbelief. Trevor was just here a few days ago, and now he was gone? I felt completely numb. This couldn't have happened. It must've been a bad dream. I'd probably wake up in the morning. I'd have to wake up from this, right?

Services and stuff were scheduled for Tuesday, so I talked to my mom about school that week. We agreed it might be good if I went in on Monday just to keep my mind busy because I might need to take off the rest of the week. I went through the motions on Monday, but the strangest thing is that I didn't say a word, nor did I hear a sound. Honestly. I didn't hear one thing the whole school day. It was like the world around me was on "mute." Maybe I was in denial. I felt like I was in some crazy parallel universe, and I kept replaying what had happened over and over again in my head. I didn't notice anyone else talking about it, so I guessed the news wasn't out yet. Then again, with the state Mr. Nolan had been in, I wouldn't have been surprised if he hadn't notified the school yet. And I sure as hell wasn't saying anything about it.

That day, I decided to walk home instead of taking the bus. I was one of those kids who lived right on the border, so I did have a bus assigned to get to and from school, but I was close enough to walk if I wanted. It was nice out on Monday; the sun was bright and seemed to be smiling. It felt cruel given the circumstances—almost like the sun was sneering at the situation.

I rounded the corner a block from the school building only to see Manny, and three others of his crew, looking shady as usual.

"You Petey?" Manny asked, somewhat ominously. I laughed inwardly, wondering what this guy's IQ was. I had met him before. Had he forgotten who I was?

"Who's asking?" I responded, trying to appear confident. These guys did make me nervous though.

"We are," he said stepping closer. "Trevor owes us money. Aren't you a friend of his?"

"Um, you guys didn't hear?" A couple of the guys shuffled their feet. They definitely looked strung out on something.

"No, we heard, but that doesn't change facts. He owes us money."

"Well, I don't know what to tell you. He's dead. I'm pretty sure he can't get the money to you."

"Don't be a dick," he said threateningly. "You're one of his friends. Don't think we won't come after *you* for it. We could beat your ass right now." That was a good point. It *was* four against one. They obviously had an advantage. I tried not to look fazed.

"I'll see what I can do," I lied. "But I gotta go." I threw my shoulders back, trying to look bigger than I was, and then side-stepped around them, moving as briskly down the sidewalk as I could without breaking into a run. I kept thinking about wolves. If I started to run, I reasoned, they might run after me. But if I just walked assertively, maybe they'd let me go.

They did. I moved as quickly as I could, and when I was out of sight, I started to run. Did that seriously just happen? Of all the days

I decided to *walk* home—the day after Trevor *died*—his posse comes after me looking for fucking drug money? Maybe I really *was* in an alternate universe. I assumed they were desperate for more money and more drugs. I had heard stories of people going to ridiculous lengths just to scrape together enough cash to get their next high. Unreal.

As I got closer to my house, I was pretty out of breath, so I sat down on the curb and put my head between my knees. My heart was pounding. I seriously couldn't take much more. I felt utterly broken and hopeless. Completely alone. Really, honestly, think about it—I had no one. I never felt so awful in my life. The word *broken* kept repeating in my head. I started to think of everyone I knew and how seriously broken everyone was.

Take my mom, for example. Her husband dies when I'm three and then she's stuck alone raising a kid by herself. So she marries Ricky—a complete asshole who cheats on her and fights with her son all the time. Then there's Trevor—this kid who loses his mom on 9/11 and has been fucked up ever since. He gets into drugs to cope with the sadness and dies. That's two out of three Nolans dead now. Then there's Trevor's dad, who loses his wife on 9/11 and focuses on work and whatever new flavor of the week he can get so he won't have to deal with the unbearable pain of being a single parent trying to raise a fucked-up son—who's dead now, by the way. And how about Ms. Moore? Or should I call her "Ms. *Less*"? The teacher who we all used to rely on who can't be there for us because…? I don't even *know* why. I guess the school system is keeping her busy. And me? I'm a kid whose dad died when I was three, whose mom remarried a complete bum (who used to beat me, but nevertheless she recently chose over me), whose girl interest moved away, whose new best friend died (for which I'll probably be traumatized forever by having discovered his lifeless body), whose teacher abandoned him, and who really has no one else left in the world who cares about him. Yup, *broken*. Broken, broken, broken. Every last one of us. God, why was I even *here* anymore? What the hell was the *point* of any of this? I didn't even have the tears left to cry. I just continued to feel numb.

I stood up from the curb and started to jog back toward the school. I'm not sure why, but I was hoping that maybe Ms. Moore was still there—that maybe she could see me and help me make sense of all of this. I needed someone. I needed something. I mean, she'd *have* to make time for this, wouldn't she? It was an emergency. I was desperate.

I ran so fast you would've thought I was trying out for the Olympic team. I prayed the whole way there that I wouldn't run into Manny and Co. again. When I got to the building, I ran to her classroom first. Lights out, door locked. No surprise there. But she was always in meetings and stuff lately, so maybe she was in the building somewhere, just not in her room. I tried to will it so. Maybe my wishing and hoping would make it happen. I headed for the main office. When I got there, I leaned over the desk of the first secretary I saw.

"Is Ms. Moore here?" I asked, out of breath. "Please?" I begged.

"Oh, I'm sorry, hon—she's at a conference all day today for the NASA testing. You know, they're really pushing for high test scores this year," she said smiling, oblivious.

*High test scores?* That was actually comical considering what I was going through at that moment.

"Ok," I said breathing out, not even hiding my disappointment. I trudged home, my head spinning. At that moment, I envied Trevor. He was so lucky. He didn't have to feel the pain I did. It was excruciating. I didn't know how much more I could take. Joining Trevor sounded pretty good right about now.

# CHAPTER 22

I had thought more about what Will had said. Maybe it really *was* time to pack it in. The conference I had gone to on Monday left me even more discouraged. It was all about NASA testing, and the workshop's purpose was to go over what I would personally call the "five S's": structure, scheduling, security measures, scores, and stakes (very *high* stakes, I might add). You wouldn't believe it all if I told you, but I'll share just one glittering gem so you get the idea. These kinds of standardized tests always required high security. A teacher could lose his or her license if a kid brought a cell phone or something in to the test (I especially loved noting that it was always the teacher's fault). Since this test would be computer-based and the first of its kind, the stakes were even higher with internet access, chances of cheating, etc. We were informed that if a kid got sick during the test and vomited or something, we'd have to bag it up as evidence and send it to the State Department for proof. The absurdity of it at least made me smile to myself. Nothing surprised me anymore.

Sitting next to me at the conference was a woman from another district and a student-teacher who was under her tutelage for the semester. The poor kid looked so frightened at the prospect of losing his teaching license before he even officially had it. I hadn't even thought of kids who were just going in to the profession now. Poor things. They'd never know how good it used to be before all this. If I were his mother, I probably would have discouraged him from going into teaching nowadays. I couldn't even believe I had these thoughts, but it was the truth.

When I arrived to school Tuesday morning, I got there earlier than usual. The day after being absent, I always tried to get there earlier since there was typically a mess left behind from whatever substitute had covered me. While I was signing in, Andrea, one of the office secretaries, perked up.

"Good morning, Ms. Moore. There was a boy here after school yesterday—said he was looking for you."

*Petey.* The thought of him made my stomach twist. I nodded and hustled off to my classroom. I had been thinking of him all weekend, even at the conference. Something didn't feel right. I looked at my schedule for the day and commanded myself to pencil in his name during my lunch. The thought of "penciling in" a kid made me sick. That had never been the case. I used to think of connecting with kids as a job *requirement*. Now it was only a "luxury" if you could "squeeze them in" to your corporate executive schedule. It was as though they were no longer central to the job—they were just superfluous fluff. The time had come where I needed a personal secretary for all these "humans" I had to deal with. I shook my head. How insane. *Ok, that's what I'll do. I'll go and find him today at lunch. Then I'll be able to check on him.* I flicked on my computer and checked my e-mail. That was another thing I had come to dread as a teacher. It never failed that some ominous message would be waiting for us in our e-mail. It never failed.

Sure enough, I had an e-mail from Ellen, one of the vice principals. She informed me that she needed to observe me sometime that week or next, so we would have to schedule a pre-observation meeting. Of course she had sent the e-mail first thing Monday morning while I was at the conference, so I figured she'd already be annoyed that I hadn't gotten back to her immediately. (Did they even check the schedule to see who was out on a given day? It's not like I had *volunteered* to go to the stupid conference. I had been *sent*—by her office). I sighed and rolled my eyes. I had to teach all morning and wouldn't have a break till lunch. Maybe I could e-mail her back while simultaneously teaching. I'm sure that's what was expected. Regardless, I had to find Petey at lunch. I had to make sure he was ok. I felt terrible that he had come looking for me, and I hadn't been there. I thought of all the times in the past year or two that the same thing had probably happened. It made me even more resentful about the way things were in education now.

At lunch, I went to the gym to see if Petey had gone to play basketball. He could usually be found there on the flex period. My heels click-clacked on the wooden floor as I walked through the gym. It seemed to make kids stop, stare, and tense up a bit. That was the one place where you could usually rely on not hearing the "authorities' arrival"-sounding noise. I was pleased to see faces relax as they saw it was only me trekking through.

"Hey, Danny!" I called to one of the boys who often played basketball with Petey. "Have you seen Petey today? I thought he might be here shooting hoops with you."

"No!" he shouted back over the noise in the gym. "He's in my first period class, but he wasn't there today. I think he's absent."

*Absent.* No way. Petey was never absent. He had the best attendance of any kid I had ever seen. Even though he was never an Honors student, that kid never missed a day of school. He actually had great attendance. "Thanks!" I yelled back, turning on my heel and heading out.

I hoofed it to the attendance office, and poked my head in. "Hi, Sue," I said, waving to the attendance secretary. "Can you tell me if Petey Guzman is here today?"

"Sure," she replied, starting to click away on her computer. "Umm…it looks like he's out today. Why? Does he usually cut your class?" she asked, smiling.

"Oh. Uh, no, I don't even have him this year. I was just looking for him. Thanks," I replied, starting down the hall. *Oh, no,* I thought. *Something's gotta be wrong.* That kid was never absent.

"Ms. Moore!" I heard a voice call. I turned around. It was Ellen, the vice principal. "I was hoping we could meet for your pre-ob meeting if you have some time right now," she said pointedly, in a more telling than asking way. I groaned inwardly. For goodness' sake—it was lunch. And I was hungry. Then I remembered how she was holding my overall worth and value as a teacher in her hands— along with a little scoresheet (*and her little dog, too,* I thought to myself). Accommodating her was probably a good idea if I wanted to keep my job. (Although at this rate, I wasn't so sure anymore).

"Sure," I smiled cheerfully. "Would you like to come to my classroom now?"

# CHAPTER 23

So, that's where I'm at right now. I attended the wake for Trevor on Tuesday, and then the funeral Wednesday morning. My mom came Tuesday night to the later viewing. I was there all day for both of them. (Ricky didn't come at all, but I'm sure you figured that). My mom had an early shift on Wednesday, so she couldn't make the funeral, but I was there of course. I've actually been home from school this whole week. You know what the strange thing is? I've been holed up all week, and other than eating or showering, the *only* thing I've been doing is writing. Before the school year started, I had gotten a new notebook expecting to continue journaling with Ms. Moore again this fall. But after she told me she wasn't accepting any new kids' journals, I kinda didn't wanna write to her anymore. It was like a silent protest. I felt like, if you're not gonna do it for them, then I'm not submitting to you anymore. It was probably childish, but I just felt like she was so far gone, there wasn't any point anymore.

I don't wanna say I was disappointed in her the most, but I guess I was. I mean, Trevor was kinda always fucked up, so I could almost get that his life would end in a pretty sad way. And I never expected my mom to choose Ricky over me, but I guess she's been through a lot and she was always the peacemaker type, so I probably wouldn't put it past her. But really, who else was there for me? Everyone I expected to be able to rely on, I no longer could. I guess I felt the biggest loss was Ms. Moore because she was a *teacher*. She had told us she'd always be there for us. I mean, wasn't that part of her job description? Wasn't she paid to care about us? And I know that when she said it back then, it had been genuine. She wasn't a bull-shitter. But for the life of me, I couldn't understand what had happened— why she wasn't there for us anymore. All I knew was that she wasn't. (And honestly, when you looked around my school, it kinda seemed like *every* teacher was just "too busy" for us kids). When I really thought about it, though, I kinda didn't blame the actual teachers. I blamed the school system. It was like they had made *all* the teachers too busy to care—or too busy to have *time* to care. What a crock. I thought schools were supposed to *support* students.

Anyway, I've been writing just for me. My own therapy, I guess. It's weird how, even though I felt like Ms. Moore was so far gone, she was still influencing me. She had always told us that when all else fails, *write*. Just write everything down that you're feeling. That somehow, it *is* therapeutic, and that there *is* a purpose in getting everything out. So since Tuesday, I've been writing all of this— everything that's happened since my freshman year. I kept my notebook with me at Trevor's services, and whenever there was down time, or I was just trying to distract myself, I wrote. Since I've been home, too, I've been writing nonstop—everything from Ms. Moore's class freshman year, to all the Ricky secrets, to the fight with Josh (which seems like ages ago), to watching Kelsey leave, to meeting Trevor, to disowning my mom, to *burying* Trevor, to the druglords confronting me, to realizing Ms. Moore *is* "no more."

And the truth is, I'm not mad, I'm not sad, I'm just numb. And I feel so done. I'm just sick of all of this. I mean, what is the *point* of even being here? Is life just one big fucked-up struggle that never amounts to anything? I mean, when I look back at the fight with Josh, it's so stupid. But it seemed so important back then. Little did I know how out of control everything would get. I'm just so *tired*. I'm exhausted from all of it. Ya know, I'm supposed to take some crazy-ass computer test later this year, too…the NASA or something? Yeah, cuz I'm sure I really care about ace-ing *that* thing with all of the other shit that's going on in my life.

So, it's Sunday morning right now as I write this sentence. It's been very quiet in my house lately. No one's really been talking at all. I practically never hear a sound anymore. I don't know what's going on with my mom and Ricky, and I honestly don't care. I'm over it. I think he's been groveling for the last week or so. They're supposed to be going out for a "romantic dinner" tonight. That really translates to more "I'm Sorrys" and "It'll Be Different Nows." I'm glad I'll be home alone tonight.

I don't even think they'd miss me if I were gone. Really, who would it matter to if I wasn't here? Probably Trevor. But he's already gone. Maybe Ms. Moore. But would she even notice? I bet those druglords would notice. They'd still wanna hustle me for money. I've actually been kind of scared being home the last few days, cuz let's face it: it's only a matter of time before they come after me again.

I've felt this way before. It's like the world is just slipping away. Like it's sliding out from underneath me. I don't really see the point of being here anymore. Maybe I'm depressed. I don't know what you'd call it. But I wanted to write everything down. I wanted it to be read. I just want someone to understand what the hell happened, how everything got so fucked up, how I had no choice.

I filled up this whole notebook with most of the highlights and timeline of events, sparing you some of the details from the stories I wrote in Ms. Moore's journals. I figured that if there's something you need more detail on, you can get it from those entries. In the end, I guess I want someone to find these—to know my story, to read it, to get it. Who knows? Maybe someone will publish it one day, and then other kids could relate to me and what happened. Maybe other kids out there feel the same way I do. Maybe they'll understand why I did what I had to do.

I mean, I miss Trevor. I miss confiding in him. I miss being able to tell him some of the dark shit—like what Ricky did all those years or how unfair it was that both our parents died on 9/11. When we talked, I felt so much better. I felt normal.

I miss my mom, too. I am so angry that she never bothered finding out the truth—that in the end, she didn't choose *me*. But I still love her. And I miss her.

I miss my dad. My real dad. I really do. And I know it's stupid to be pissed that he died cuz he didn't do it on purpose, but I still miss him. My life would've been a whole lot different with him in it, I think. It would've been so nice to have a real dad.

And I miss Ms. Moore. I miss her pink comments all over my journals. I miss her telling me that my feelings were ok—that they made sense and that I wasn't a total fuck-up. Even though she wasn't a fan of blue ink, she still read my entries anyway. Man, I really miss her. I miss our talks, our journals, and most of all, I miss her being able to be there for me.

So, I'm signing off now. But I wanted you to have my story. Maybe someone can get it to Ms. Moore—if she's not too busy to read it.

# CHAPTER 24

My observation with Ellen was set for the following Monday morning. (Of course she had to reschedule from Friday to Monday because "something came up" in her office. I loved how these administrators could always do things on *their* terms because their time and schedule was more important than ours. But if a teacher ever had to reschedule, we'd be clapped in the stocks, I'm sure). Needless to say, I had spent the entire week worrying about being perfect for Friday, only to be rescheduled for Monday; hence, the weekend was spent preparing and worrying and grinding my teeth at night. I couldn't *wait* for Monday to be over.

I noticed that the school was pretty quiet that morning while I was setting up my classroom. I hadn't gotten there as early as I would've liked for the day of an observation scheduled for first period, but the building was noticeably empty. It was like a ghost town. I started wondering if the staff was just so fed up with the way things were, that maybe they were just "clocking in" and "clocking out" to the minute of the scheduled work day. Maybe they had had enough.

Moving desks around made pretty obnoxious, screeching noises on the floor in my room that reverberated against the walls. But over the noise, I could still somehow hear incredibly loud shrieking coming from the hallway. I thought I was hearing things until I jumped about two feet in the air from the incessant banging I suddenly heard on my classroom door. An attractive, yet hysterical woman frantically pressed her nose into the glass pane of my door, her little hand waving around a notebook. She looked vaguely familiar to me, but she definitely seemed to know who I was.

"Ms. Moore! Ms. Moore!" she shouted so loudly the glass vibrated. "Open up! Oh, God! Dios mío!"

At that, I rushed to the door and opened it for the woman. She fell into me, dead weight, dropping to her knees. "Please help me! Please help! Oh, God! My son! My precious *son!*" she screamed, tears spewing from her eyes. The notebook she was holding dropped to the floor, landing on its spine, the book's pages opening wide. It was then that I saw the familiar blue ink.

*Oh, my God. Petey.* "Mrs. Guzman, what is this? What's happened?" I screamed back panicked, holding the upper half of her body against mine. But I didn't have to ask. As she wailed and wept, I already knew.

"He's gone! He's gone! Last night! Dios mío! Oh, my *GOD!*" she panted.

It felt like the earth was sliding out from underneath me. I thought I was going to faint, but somehow I remained standing. A little yellow note had fluttered to the floor when the notebook had dropped. As I held Mrs. Guzman, I was able to make out Petey's blue hieroglyphics.

*Mom, I'm sorry we fought. I forgive both of us. Went to go be with Dad and Trevor. I love you always. Your son, Petey. P.S. Please give this notebook to Ms. Moore.*

"Is he dead?" I asked bluntly, even though I knew the answer. She nodded, her face buried in my stomach. "Suicide?" I asked painfully, tears spilling over my lower lids, sliding down my face. She nodded again, and the smell of her perfumed-hair wafted up to my nose. I thought of the many times Petey must've smelled this scent—and how now, he never would again.

I held Mrs. Guzman for several minutes as we both wept. Sometimes she would shudder in the way you do when you're trying to gasp for air between sobs. When she started to quiet, she whispered very softly, "This notebook is specifically for you. He said so. I only read a few pages of it. But it looks like it's his story of everything that led up to this. We found him last night. He…" her voice trailed off. "This was on his bed with the note on top of it. His final journal to you…and the world," she finished, a gurgling noise coming from her throat.

I didn't know what to do, what to say, what to think. I just stood there. And held Petey's mother. And cried with her. *This is all my fault. I wasn't there for him. He had no one to go to. This poor kid. He had no one to go to all because I was worried about this stupid job.* It was in that moment then, that nothing was important anymore. Not SAAs, not NASAs, not the Michaels Model, not observations, not test scores, not *anything* that these leaders kept saying would "improve education." Really? At what cost? A kid was *dead* on their watch. All at once, a million feelings coursed through my body. I was so angry at the system. *This* was the product that they had created.

This kid was *dead* because no one had the *time* to keep him from falling through the cracks. And here I was, holding in my arms the innocent boy's inconsolable mother.

I should've known how bad it was. I should've sensed how depressed Petey was. I had even gone to find him, but then it was observation time again, and that was looming over me, and I didn't get a chance to seek him out. I wondered how many other kids felt so abandoned by their teachers. Maybe it was silly to blame myself, but I did. And even more so, I resented the school system for how they had contributed, for the part they had played in this. Because they *did*. They had a *huge* part in this.

After what seemed like hours, Mrs. Guzman stood up and dusted off the knees of her pants. She walked over to the tissue box, patted her eyes, and blew her nose two separate times.

"I'm sorry to have to tell you this way," she said, barely audible. "But you were so involved with him. You knew him so *well*."

I felt so guilty when she said that. The truth was, I *didn't* know him that well anymore because I had been spread too thin to invest the time in him I originally had. Time that he had so obviously, desperately needed. Time that was too late to get back now.

"I was hoping maybe we could grieve together and try to make some sense of this. I know we both loved him very much," she said, her accent more apparent now. "After you read his story, will you return it to me? This note is all he left for me," she continued, clutching the yellow piece of paper, her tiny fingers trembling.

I nodded silently and she went on to discuss how she was planning services for later in the week. Everything was happening in such a whirlwind, my head felt like it was spinning in full rotations from upside down to right side up, as though I were on a sickening theme park ride. She finally headed for the classroom door just as the morning bell signaled the start of the day. That meant homeroom students would begin trickling in at any moment.

I headed over to the tissue box, and started to wipe my face. I felt so sick that a little vomit started to climb up my throat, but I forcefully swallowed it back down.

"Ms. Moore!" a syrupy-sweet voice called. I spun around. It was Ellen, clipboard and observation paperwork in tow. "I hope you don't mind I'm a little early. This way I'll get to observe you from the *moment* your class begins," she said cheerfully, plopping herself down at a student desk in the back of the room.

Will had been right, as usual. It was time to leave this profession altogether.

# CHAPTER 25

So I know this would normally be where you would read a chapter from Petey, since we've been alternating this whole time. But as you know, he's no longer here. And so the very last chapter is up to me... I now believe my purpose here was to publish Petey Guzman's story because I believe it's too important not to hear—and not to heed. I am hoping that everyone who reads his story will learn from it. When I pieced it together, I took entries from his final journal and threaded them in with mine. (I hope he doesn't mind that I did this, but our stories were so parallel, I wanted him and all of his readers to understand what was happening on both sides. I still have Petey's "blood on my hands"; I know I am partially to blame for his death. But I was hoping that by including what was going on simultaneously in *both* of our lives, readers would get the full story. I hope and pray that somehow, some way, Petey can learn the truth about how and why he ended up feeling so abandoned).

As you know, Petey's handwriting was so terrible, it could've been mistaken for a doctor's. Back when he was a sophomore, Petey said he would never be smart enough to become a doctor, but I beg to differ. He actually may have discovered a *cure* to the sickness in education: which is, we need the focus to be *back* on our kids so we don't lose one more of them. Let us learn from the lesson *Petey* taught us (and here I thought *I* was the teacher). Petey was the best teacher of all, actually. But the lesson he taught me was probably the hardest one I've ever learned in my life.

I'm sorry that it was *Petey* who had to be the one to teach us all this very important lesson. But sharing his story was the only way I thought we could honor his memory *enough*—to illustrate that his life *did* have a purpose and that he *did* leave a legacy. His life was sacrificed by the school system. And what a price we will have to pay—for him, and any other student we choose to lose while we are too busy crunching numbers, looking at data, raising test scores, and observing teachers all in the name of "improving education."

And I'm sure "leaders" in the field will deny it. They'll say it wasn't their fault—that Petey was depressed, that this would've happened anyway. They'll pass the blame on to something else and go back to compiling their test scores. And the point is, they've completely *missed* the point. They don't even *get* the point. The point is, there *is* no point to any of this if we're not doing what's in the best interest of our kids. Didn't most people go in to education to *help* kids? To be there for *kids*? If we're kept too busy to catch the warning signs of a kid who's hurting, then I say the system is broken…and pointless.

So I wanted to publish this for Petey's sake, as a way to honor him posthumously. I am hoping that somehow he will *know* the legacy he left, and how *proud* I am of him. He wrote enough to make a whole *book*. He *did* write a book; I just helped put it together. I only fused in my recollections so that you all could have the full story, seeing it from both sides. Maybe one day, we can publish *all* of his journals for the world to see—the ones he wrote to me over his three high school years. I remember saying to him during the first marking period of his freshman year, "You have a lot to say, and you have an important story to tell." I had no idea then how true those words would be. I only wish now that he could see his impact on the world, on me, on everyone who reads his story. I am sure you are a fan of his. I am sure you think of him as fondly as I do. And I am certain that if you have read his story, and you take a moment to create a picture of him in your mind, you *smile*—just as I do.

We teachers *used* to be able to reach kids in our profession. Today, however, we've been forced to do things differently…which is why the public school system was able to claim Petey Guzman's life. I beg those of you who have read our story to heed our advice. Things *must* change in education. Teachers need to be able to do their jobs the way we used to be able to—the way teaching was intended. We need our teachers *now more than ever* today. Maybe then kids won't slip through the cracks the way Petey did. There are *good people* who want to be there for kids, who *want* to help them and inspire them. But we can't do that honorable work when our hands are tied, when we are left spinning our wheels, when we are not supported, and when we are simply forced to be a slave to a broken system. Parents, policymakers, administrators, politicians: *please* allow our teachers to reach kids. They need us. They need loving, supportive teachers in their lives who have the luxury of *time* to invest in their young lives. Please make sure Petey Guzman's short life was not taken in vain. He is counting on you. And so am I.

# Author's Note

Though the novel is fiction, the author has observed or experienced firsthand or through colleagues most of the events that occur in this story. The demise of the necessary student-teacher connection is one of the many casualties the author has witnessed over her many years in education. Hults Elko's hope is that the message in her book may be the first of several steps in the right direction for improving public education.

"We've lost sight of what *really* matters in today's classrooms—and teachers and students *sense* this, *feel* this, and are absorbing the impact (perhaps at a level even below their awareness). The human connection between teachers and students is being driven out of classrooms, and being replaced by inconsequential, irrelevant, nonessential, insignificant, unimportant demands and requirements (driven by a larger agenda). It's time to face this issue head-on and do what's *right* for today's students."

"Gone are the days of relationships, rapport, and classroom community within our schools. I grieve the losses of these and stand by today's teachers who strive to overcome this adversity and continue to press on, emphasizing innovation, creativity, and *teacher*-determined 'best practices' within their classrooms. Many fail to recognize that teachers are *professionals* who carefully hone their craft and are truly *experts* at knowing their students *and* their needs. It is a noble profession that is not fit for everybody. Teaching is an *art*, not a science. It is never perfect, but it *is* marvelous and beautiful. It can't be quantified in numbers."

"Today's students deserve the *best* from their teachers—teachers who are not inhibited, hindered, or shackled by the demands placed on them. *Please* let teachers do their jobs—jobs which have always been about connecting with, and *inspiring* the children in their classrooms."

~All my love, hope, and appreciation to today's teachers and students, E.A. Hults Elko

CPSIA information can be obtained
at www.ICGtesting.com
Printed in the USA
FFOW04n1104021015
17381FF